OUT OF REACH

David stared at Jade, his happy expression fading. "What's wrong with you?" he managed to ask her.

Jade put her hands on her hips and glared at him. "What's wrong with me is that I don't happen to appreciate you breaking a confidence. You told me you wouldn't say a word to anybody!"

"Yeah, and I didn't." David was staring right back at her.

"Yeah, right. Then how come Amy Sutton and Lila just *happen* to have found out?"

David's eyes sparkled with anger. "Look, Jade, either you trust me or you don't. I swear that I didn't tell a single soul your little secret, ridiculous as I think it is."

"It's not ridiculous!" Jade shrieked. "David, you're the most insensitive, the most—"

David broke in, his own voice getting louder. "Who's insensitive? You're the one who's ashamed of your own family!" He stared at her indignantly. "There's something wrong with your attitude, Jade. That's the real problem."

"Thank you very much, but I don't need you to tell me what my problem is," Jade said coldly.

David walked past her. "I want to know why you can't face up to who you are, Jade. You know, until you do, you're going to have nothing but problems!"

Jade felt her eyes fill with tears. She reached out her hand to grab David's arm, but there was no stopping him.

Bantam Books in the Sweet Valley High Series
Ask your bookseller for the books you have missed

SWEET VALLEY HIGH

OUT OF REACH

Written by
Kate William

Created by
FRANCINE PASCAL

BANTAM BOOKS
TORONTO · NEW YORK · LONDON · SYDNEY · AUCKLAND

RL 6, IL age 12 and up

OUT OF REACH
A Bantam Book / November 1988

Sweet Valley High is a registered trademark of Francine Pascal.

Conceived by Francine Pascal.

Produced by Daniel Weiss Associates, Inc.,
27 West 20th Street, New York, NY 10011

Cover art by James Mathewuse

ISBN 0-553-27596-8

Published simultaneously in the United States and Canada

Bantam Books are published by Bantam Books, a division of Bantam Doubleday Dell Publishing Group, Inc. Its trademark, consisting of the words "Bantam Books" and the portrayal of a rooster, is Registered in U.S. Patent and Trademark Office and in other countries. Marca Registrada. Bantam Books, 666 Fifth Avenue, New York, New York 10103.

PRINTED IN THE UNITED STATES OF AMERICA

O   0 9 8 7 6 5 4 3 2 1

OUT OF REACH

One

"I'm so excited about the show!" Amy Sutton exclaimed, her gray eyes shining. "Don't you think I'm just perfect for the solo part?"

It was lunchtime, and several girls were crowded around a table in the cafeteria, discussing Sweet Valley High's upcoming music and dance show, which was being staged to raise money to start a dance program so that students could take modern dance or ballet as an elective.

"I haven't heard much about it," Cara Walker said. "What kind of acts are they going to have? I don't remember there ever being a show like that here before."

"Ms. Bellasario's directing it," Amy answered, glancing at Jessica. "Only no one knows yet who's going to take over as student producer now that Maria Santelli had to drop out." Maria, one of the cheerleaders, had to give up her position when she got very ill with the flu. "Anyway, there are going to be auditions the day after tomorrow—that's Wednesday, right? Supposedly Ms. Bellasario wants to have a lot of different acts, though dance is most important. I think The Droids are going to play one of their songs, and some musical numbers—you know, people playing instruments and stuff." Her eyes gleamed. "But the big solo before the grand finale is being reserved for a really good dancer. And that's what I want to get!"

Jessica Wakefield looked skeptically at her friend. As much as she liked Amy, she had to agree with her twin, Elizabeth, that Amy had an inflated sense of her own worth. Jessica had spent enough time on the cheerleading squad with Amy to suspect she wasn't as great a dancer as she thought she was. Personally, Jessica wasn't interested in dancing right now. Recently she had tried out for a role in the school production of *You Can't Take It with You*, but instead of winning the glamorous lead, she ended up with the part of a comic character, whose dancing was terrible. Also, she didn't feel like

2

getting involved in another production where she would have to spend every waking minute working on it. Even though her twin sister Elizabeth was in charge of publicity, Jessica wasn't going to audition. The play had been fun, but she had a lot of other things to do. With cheerleading, Pi Beta Alpha—the exclusive sorority she was president of—and A.J., her brand-new boyfriend, she had her hands full.

However, if Amy really wanted to be in the show, Jessica wasn't going to try to talk her out of it.

"I bet you'd be great for the solo," she murmured, not looking directly at Amy.

Lila Fowler was less polite. "I don't want to hurt your feelings or anything, Amy, but there's going to be an awful lot of competition for the big dance solo." She tossed her hair back. "I had a discussion with Ms. Bellasario about it yesterday. Lots of people are going to be auditioning."

"Like who?" Amy demanded, undaunted.

"Well, probably Jade Wu." Lila, the richest girl in Sweet Valley, liked being the person who always knew what was going on at school. "I told you about her before, remember? She happens to be an incredible dancer. I bet you anything she gets the solo part." She gave Amy an imperious look. Lila tended to be competitive, and there was a natural rivalry between her and Amy. "I hear Jade Wu is practically a professional."

Amy looked scornful. "But you told me Jade's only a sophomore," she said disparagingly.

Jessica laughed. "So what? If she's the best for the part, Ms. Bellasario will give it to her for sure."

Amy stuck out her lower lip in a pout. "But she's Chinese! She doesn't look right for the part. The soloist for the finale should be blond, all-American—like me."

"Jade's American," Lila observed wryly. "Just because her father was born in China doesn't mean she isn't American. I think you'd better plan to audition for the chorus line." She giggled. "Or maybe you and Jessica could try singing something together. Like 'Row, row, row your boat.' "

Jessica barely listened to Amy's angry response. Actually, she hadn't heard from her sister yet whether Jade was trying out for the solo role. Elizabeth might know, since she had thrown herself into the production with characteristic energy. It would be interesting to watch and see what happened if Jade *did* compete with Amy!

Jessica had been curious more than once about the beautiful, petite sophomore. Jade had only moved to Sweet Valley a few months ago, and she was a shy, delicate girl who kept to herself. The one thing everyone at school had heard about Jade was that she was a phenomenal dancer. She wanted to be a professional ballerina one day, and from what Jessica had heard, she seemed to have a real shot at it—she was that good. Jessica wondered if her twin knew anything more about Jade. Just at that moment Elizabeth came hurrying over to the table. "You guys aren't going to believe it," she said excitedly. "You know Maria Santelli had to drop out of the show. Well, guess who just got drafted to take her place?"

Everyone stared at Elizabeth in surprise.

"Me!" Elizabeth exclaimed with a rueful laugh. "Ms. Bellasario wants *me* to be the student producer of the show!"

Elizabeth hadn't intended to get herself into such a big job. But the show had to go on. And as always, Elizabeth was ready to help out in a pinch!

Jade was sitting at a corner table in the cafeteria across from Melanie Forman, her best friend. Melanie, who was also a sophomore, had a great sense of humor, and Jade really enjoyed her company. Today especially she was happy to have her friend's support, because all she could think about was how unfair it was that she couldn't audition for the upcoming show.

"I can't believe you're not even going to give it a shot," Melanie objected. "Come on, Jade. You know you're the best dancer in the whole school."

Jade pushed her silky black hair over her shoulder. "What difference would it make? You know my dad would never let me dance in public. I'd have to give up the part as soon as I got it—*if* I got it." She sighed. "I talked to Eve about the show. She thinks I'd be perfect for the solo." Eve Miller was Jade's dance teacher. For the past six years Jade had been studying ballet. But she had only worked with Eve since her family moved to Sweet Valley. The lessons were a present from her grandparents, who knew Jade's dream was to be a ballerina one day. Jade could still remember what they had said to her the day she turned nine. "If this is your dream, we'll help you reach it." Ever since then, they had lived up to their promise. If only her parents were as supportive as her grandparents were!

Jade's dark eyes were sad as she said, "I wish I had parents like yours, Melanie. Your family lets you do whatever you want. If only my father understood how much dancing means to me . . ."

Melanie frowned. "Well, it's true my parents aren't as strict as yours. But your parents have such interesting backgrounds. I love listening to their stories. When your father starts talking about what it was like to grow up in China . . ."

Jade sat up straight, and tossed her napkin onto her tray. "I'm sick to death of hearing him go on about it. You'd think he still lived in China! Well, he doesn't. He's an American now. So's my mother, and so am I. My father insists on living in the past. Every second word that comes out of his mouth is about China. In China girls wear their hair like this. In China people take their vacations at such-and-such. If we lived in China, we wouldn't do this or that. I can't stand it!"

Melanie was quiet for a minute. "But you must be proud of them, Jade. Not everyone has parents as fascinating as yours."

Jade shook her head vehemently. "Believe me, I'd give anything in the world if I could swap with you, Mel. My parents are *wonderful*, but it's impossible to live with them and still lead a normal life." She frowned. "I can't do anything other kids my age can. I'm not allowed to date. I can't even spend a night over at your house, or have you come over to stay with me. And why can't I? Because in China girls don't sleep over at their friends' houses. I guess it's worse because I'm an only child, too. If I had brothers and sisters, they wouldn't pay so much attention to me. But as it is . . . Mel, I feel so trapped."

Jade knew how distraught and angry she sounded, but she couldn't help herself. For as long as she could remember, she and her father had disagreed about almost everything that mattered. Jade wanted to be American in every way. She wanted American clothes, American food, American friends. If she could *look* American, she would be overjoyed. But Jade was the epitome of Oriental beauty. She was small, delicate, with skin as smooth as ivory, beautiful dark eyes, and jet-black hair as fine as silk. She knew her father loved her and that he just wanted to make sure she maintained her ties with Chinese culture. He distrusted Americans, and he wanted Jade to form friendships with other Chinese-Americans like herself—not with girls like Melanie.

Dr. Wu had come to America when he was twenty-three. After studying for his Ph.D. in physics at CalTech, he had worked in California, first as a professor, then as a business consultant. Six months ago he had been transferred from San Francisco to a new branch office that was opening in Sweet Valley, and the Wus made the move.

It had been a mixed blessing for the whole family. On the plus side, Mrs. Wu's parents, the Sungs, lived in Sweet Valley. Jade was finally going to have the chance to spend some time with her grandparents. But each of them missed San Francisco. Dr. Wu missed Chinatown and the close Chinese friendships he had developed there. Mrs. Wu felt uprooted, and Jade missed the dance community. She'd had a wonderful dance class in San Francisco, and even the lessons her grandparents set up for her with Eve Miller didn't make up for it.

In fact, it had been a tough adjustment all the way around. In San Francisco Jade had managed to build up a network of friends—some Chinese, some American—whom her father grudgingly accepted. The move had only brought their differences out in the open again. Dr. Wu was constantly worrying that Sweet Valley High was the wrong sort of atmosphere for Jade— that, as he put it, "there won't be any people like you around." Jade hated that phrase!

Not even her best friend completely understood. Yet of all the people Jade had met so far at school, Melanie was the most understanding. She seemed to guess intuitively how hard it was for Jade to get along with her father and how much Jade hated asking her mother to intervene.

"What if you just tried to talk to your father? You could explain to him how much being in the show would mean to you," Melanie suggested.

Jade shook her head impatiently. "No, it would never work. He'd say that it's OK to take private ballet lessons. At least that seems to him like some sort of strict discipline. And as long as it's private, just me and my teacher, then he can't really object to it. I mean, he doesn't support it or anything, but he doesn't forbid it." She frowned. "But it would be completely different being in a show. He wouldn't think it was 'serious dancing.' For my father everything has to be totally serious. If you're not working as hard as he works, then it just doesn't count. He doesn't respect things like dance shows."

"But this is going to be a great show!" Melanie objected. "And believe me, you'd have to work very hard, with the rehearsals and all. Jade, I can't stand to think of you not even trying out."

Jade took a deep breath. "Well, the only hope is talking to my mother about it. Even though she takes my father's side most of the time, I think she'll be more sympathetic about this. She remembers what it's like to be young, to want to do things with other people." She sighed. "But even so, I think she'll take his side. She'll think it's flashy, a waste of time, not serious enough."

"What if you asked Eve to talk to them? You know, she could tell them how much being in it could mean to your dance career. After all, every great artist needs public exposure," Melanie pointed out.

"Yeah," Jade agreed. "Maybe."

She pushed her tray away, not wanting to talk further about the show. Melanie knew her well enough not to say more. They had talked about Jade's family before, and it always came down to the same thing: a stalemate. Dr. Wu wanted one thing, and Jade wanted the opposite. And there didn't seem to be a way to close the gap between them.

Jade usually caught the downtown bus right after school to go to her dance teacher's studio. But this afternoon she missed the three-twenty bus and had to wait for the next one. She noticed a boy from her history class, David Prentiss, standing a few feet away from her. Jade had noticed him several times before. He was a really nice-looking guy. Tall—almost a foot taller than she—with sandy hair, green eyes, and freckles. He had a shy but good-hearted manner that made her look at him twice. *I'd really like to get to know him*, she thought. It was a new feeling for Jade, who had always been so busy with her dancing and studies that she hadn't even had time to look at boys.

"Hi," he said, looking at her with a shy smile. "You're Jade, aren't you? You sit behind Kevin Johnson in history class, right?"

Jade nodded. "He's as tall as you are," she said with a smile. "I can never see the black-board!"

David laughed. Just then the bus pulled up in front of them, and Jade climbed on ahead of David. There were two free seats in the back, and they sat down side by side. "I'm heading downtown," Jade explained. "I've got a dance lesson every day after school."

"Wow, that's great," David said enthusiastically. "I wish I could afford lessons." He had a cheerful, matter-of-fact air that kept his comment from seeming like a complaint. "I paint, and I'd love to be able to take a studio class. But my mom's the only one around to support all of us—we've got six kids in my family. And there just isn't any extra money for lessons."

Jade looked at him curiously. *He didn't have to tell me that,* she thought. But it made her feel good that he had. "My mother's parents pay for my lessons," she admitted. "My dad doesn't like dancing classes. If he had his way, I'd spend every afternoon at home." She blushed as soon

12

as the words were out of her mouth. It wasn't like her to say something so personal to someone she had just met. Melanie was the only friend she ever confided in, and Jade was worried how David would react.

But David didn't seem surprised or bothered by what she'd said. "Parents can be like that. I think they're especially hard on daughters." He smiled at Jade. He made her feel as if her family situation were normal, and she instantly relaxed.

"You know," David added thoughtfully as the bus turned onto the big palm-tree-lined avenue heading downtown, "you should try out for the show I'm working on. Have you heard about it? It's a show that Ms. Bellasario is directing to raise money for a dance program at school. I'm in charge of set design." He grinned. "I'm not exactly a recruiter, but I'm pretty sure we need a great dancer for a big solo number. I bet you'd be perfect."

Jade bit her lip. Wherever she turned, people were talking about the show!

"What are you doing for sets?" she asked, changing the subject as casually as possible. She didn't want to explain her reasons for not trying out.

"Well, my title is art and set director. I'm supposed to design a poster to use for advertising, and the main sets as well. I really hope you audition," he added. The bus stopped, and David stood up. "This is my stop—my house is two blocks from here. Maybe I'll see you Wednesday at the auditions," he added. He gave her a smile that made her feel warm and slightly embarrassed and happy all at the same time.

"Maybe," she murmured. Now more than ever Jade wanted to audition. She was just going to have to try her hardest to convince her parents to say yes.

Two

"Jessica!" Elizabeth called upstairs. "Am I completely crazy, or is it your night to help make dinner?"

The twins were supposed to alternate nights helping their mother with dinner because she was an interior designer and worked very long hours. But Elizabeth all too often ended up filling in for her sister. It wasn't fair, she thought now, waiting for Jessica's response. The bad thing about being the "responsible" twin was that she had to do at least twice as much of the work around the house!

It was a long-standing joke among the Wakefields that Elizabeth and Jessica were identical on the outside and totally opposite on the inside. As far as appearances were concerned, they were mirror images: they both had blond hair, blue-green eyes, slender size-six figures, and tiny dimples that showed when they smiled. Only the tiniest details distinguished them, like the fact that Elizabeth usually wore a wrist-watch and Jessica never did. Jessica operated by her own inner clock, or what her older brother, Steven, liked to call Jessica Standard Time, which meant that she basically did whatever she felt like, whenever she felt like doing it. Jessica's motto was to have fun, no matter what. And fun for Jessica meant being the center of atten-tion. Whether it was cheerleading, the sorority, or a night out at the Beach Disco, Jessica loved being in the limelight—and she usually was.

Elizabeth, on the other hand, actually liked homework and studying. She wanted to be a writer one day, so she worked long hours at *The Oracle*, Sweet Valley High's newspaper. Jes-sica couldn't believe her sister could be cooped up inside when the beautiful Southern Califor-nia coastline was so close. But the twins seemed to disagree about everything. Even now that Jessica was in love with A. J. Morgan and not playing the field, she thought her twin was too "serious" about Jeffrey French, her boyfriend. In fact, Jessica thought most of her sister's friends were on the tame side. She much preferred her own crowd, and was always trying to get her sister to see how much more fun they were than dependable, earnest people like Enid Rollins.

Elizabeth, for her part, claimed that Jessica's friends were snobby—like Lila Fowler—or boy crazy, like Amy Sutton. She tended to get impatient with her sister, especially when Jessica was shirking her responsibilities . . . as she was right now!

"I thought tonight was your night," Jessica said innocently, coming into the sunny Spanish-tiled kitchen.

"Jess!" Elizabeth exclaimed, putting her hands on her hips. "You know that I did it last night *and* the night before, when you just happened to remember a date with A.J." A.J. was a handsome redhead from Atlanta, Georgia. He had totally converted Jessica from her usual fickle, one-date-today-and-another-one-tomorrow outlook. Elizabeth thought that was great, but A.J. had also kept Jessica from doing her chores at least three days that week.

Jessica carefully avoided her sister's gaze as she strolled over to the refrigerator. "Listen," she said, opening the door and taking out salad ingredients. "You're spending all this time getting ready for the auditions for the show. Do you know whether or not Jade Wu is trying out for the solo dance role?"

"I don't know, Jess," Elizabeth admitted. "I hope she does, but I wouldn't place any bets on

17

it. Anyway, I won't know until the day of the auditions, just like everybody else."

Jessica was about to tell her twin that Amy Sutton was auditioning, when the door opened and Mr. Wakefield came in, looking tired from a long day of work at his law firm. "Hi, girls," he said, putting down his briefcase with one hand and loosening his tie with the other.

"Hi, Dad," the twins said together.

"Is your mother home yet?"

The twins shook their heads. "I'm doing dinner," Jessica announced, ignoring the dirty look Elizabeth shot her.

Mr. Wakefield walked through the house to the hall closet, where he hung up his coat. Then he regarded himself in the hallway mirror. "Look at all this gray hair," he said to himself, examining his temples. "Why didn't you two tell me I was getting old?" he asked as he came back into the kitchen. "Look how gray I am!"

"Daddy," Jessica said, "you look fantastic, and you know it. You're the youngest-looking father I know."

"Thanks," Mr. Wakefield said grimly. Actually, what Jessica said was true. Mr. Wakefield's sideburns did have a hint of gray in them, but Jessica thought they only made him look more elegant and handsome than ever. He was in excellent shape, and with his dark hair and eyes he looked years younger than he was.

"Guess what I got in the mail," he continued. "An invitation to my twenty-fifth reunion from high school. Can you believe it? I don't feel that old. Do I look that old?"

"Dad," Elizabeth said with a smile, "you look wonderful. What's wrong with a twenty-fifth-year reunion from high school? I think that's great. You and Mom can go. You'll have a fantastic time."

Mr. Wakefield sighed. "I can't go looking and feeling as middle-aged as I do. Everyone will laugh at me! If I'm going to go, I'll have to do something to make myself look younger. That's all there is to it," he said, shaking his head in despair as he left the room.

"Wow," Elizabeth said, "he sounds serious. You think he really won't go?"

"Won't go where?" Alice Wakefield asked, coming in through the back door and setting down her briefcase.

Mrs. Wakefield looked as pretty as usual. She shrugged out of her raincoat, revealing a dark blue suit beneath. With her blond hair and her bright blue eyes, she looked more like the twins' older sister than their mother.

"It's Daddy. He got an invitation to his twenty-fifth high-school reunion, and he says he doesn't want to go. He thinks he looks too old," Elizabeth explained.

"Oh, dear. I thought he'd been acting peculiar lately. Do you know he ordered an exercise bike? It's being delivered later this week," Mrs. Wakefield said with a sigh. "And he's been talking about joining a health club near work and exercising during his lunch hours. I hate to say it, but I think he may be having a mid-life crisis."

Jessica burst out laughing. "Daddy? Joining a health club? Oh, no! Don't tell me he's going to start aerobics!" She shook her head. "Maybe he'll throw out all his suits and wear jeans to the office."

"Oh, it's probably just a phase," Elizabeth said lightly. "It'll pass by the end of the week."

The twins exchanged amused glances. They couldn't feel as concerned as their mother about the situation. It seemed too funny to imagine that their father had suddenly decided he wanted to be younger!

When she got home from her dance class, Jade spent over an hour helping her mother get dinner ready. Preparing dinner together was something of a daily ritual because Dr. Wu liked traditional Chinese meals, and that meant painstaking work chopping meat and vegetables. Jade enjoyed spending the time with her mother. It gave them a chance to catch up on things, and preparing dinner relaxed her. But today she was exhausted from her workout, and just once she would have liked to have been able to go straight up to her room and call Melanie or sit down to watch TV.

Mrs. Wu was a plump, pretty woman who wore conservative Western clothes and had a shy, slightly humble manner. Although she had been born in America, Mrs. Wu still believed in old-fashioned Chinese values. She thought women should defer to their husbands, as children should to their parents. For that reason she almost always took Dr. Wu's side if he and Jade quarreled.

Still, Jade knew that any hope she had in convincing her parents to allow her to be in the show lay in getting her mother to be on her side first.

"Mother," Jade said softly, "the school is doing a big music and dance show to raise money for dance classes at school. There's a great part for a solo dancer, and I'd like to try out for it."

Mrs. Wu stared at her in consternation. "Jade, Jade," she murmured softly. "You know how your father feels about such things. He will never allow you to dance in public."

"But I want to," Jade said, trying to keep her voice from sounding defensive. "I want to get to know some of the other students." She thought of David Prentiss and blushed slightly. "I want to dance, Mother! Sooner or later Father has to understand that dancing alone is almost like not dancing at all. I need an audience. Mother, Eve thinks I'm good—good enough to be a professional."

Mrs. Wu concentrated on chopping vegetables. "Jade, you know how hard this is for me," she said. "Part of me thinks that you're right. You *should* have the chance to get to know others in your school, and you must be a good dancer to have gotten so much encouragement. But . . ." She shook her head. "I'm afraid it won't be easy convincing your father."

Jade sensed that her mother was softening. "But you could try!" she cried. "Oh, Mother, please! Please try! I'm not asking for anything more than that. But if you could talk to him . . . just try to persuade him to let me audition . . ."

Mrs. Wu sighed. "I'll try," she said, her head bent down so her daughter couldn't see the look in her eyes.

Jade felt a brief surge of hope. Maybe it would work. Maybe—just this once—she could manage to do something she really wanted to without upsetting her father.

But by the time dinner was halfway over, Jade began to lose hope. Dr. Wu was in a bad mood. Someone at work had made a slighting comment about Chinese-Americans.

"These people infuriate me," he muttered.

Jade felt her face fall. Of all the bad luck, to

have that cruel comment come today! She knew her father must have taken the insult deeply, and if she approached him now about the show, his anger would certainly work against her. She thought briefly about waiting to bring up the topic, but auditions were Wednesday, and Dr. Wu had a late meeting Tuesday night. It was now or never.

Dr. Wu continued to complain about his co-workers and their attitudes toward "our people." Finally he said, looking straight at Jade, "Can you see now how important it is for you to make Chinese friends? And you must marry a boy from China, from the province I come from if possible. It is much more gratifying and pleasurable to live with people who understand your way of life and where you come from."

Jade felt a lump form in her throat. "It isn't so bad here," she said. "There are lots of Chinese-Americans in California, Dad. Your friends, the Lees, and kids in my school. . . ." What she didn't say was that she herself wanted to get to know all kinds of people, not just Chinese-Americans. She thought of Melanie . . . and David Prentiss. It seemed so limiting to confine her friends to just one type.

Jade decided to take a chance before it was too late. She took a deep breath, then explained to her father that the music instructor was directing a show at school. She kept her comments general at first. "It's a wonderful cause," she said. "They need to raise money to start a dance program at school, and tickets will bring some of the money in. There'll be all different kinds of acts, with one long dance solo just before the grand finale." Here goes *nothing,* she told herself, taking another deep breath. "Father, I wondered how you would feel about my auditioning for the show. I would love to get that solo dancing part."

Mrs. Wu kept her eyes fixed on her plate, as if she were afraid to take part in the conversation.

Dr. Wu looked at Jade. "You want to audition in front of a whole crowded auditorium, full of people you don't know? Jade, you know how I feel about that sort of thing."

"But, Father, this is for such a good cause. And it would be so good for my dancing to have an audience. Eve thinks—"

"Would this be serious ballet dancing or that so-called modern dance?" Dr. Wu demanded.

Jade bit her lip. This was such a characteristic thing for her father to ask. Unless something was "genuine art," he didn't approve of it. The only Western music he liked was classical. He hated rock and roll, and he hated modern dance.

"It wouldn't be ballet, Father, but I'd be able to choreograph something myself, to my own taste. It'll be beautiful, I promise!"

But Dr. Wu shook his head. "Jade, I'm sorry. I don't want to disappoint you, but I really would prefer it if you wouldn't take part in this. I just don't like to think of you wasting your talent, doing some kind of strange dance in front of a group of people you don't know."

Jade felt her self-control slipping away. She kept quiet for as long as she could bear it. Then, when she was afraid she was going to start crying, she said, "Would you excuse me?" After thanking them both for dinner, Jade left the dinner table and ran up to her room. Hot tears streamed down her face.

She was sure the show was a hopeless cause. There was no way her father would ever consent.

She heard a soft tap on her door. "Jade? Can I come in?" her mother asked quietly.

Jade sat up and wiped her eyes. "It's no good," she said sadly as her mother walked into the room. "He'll never let me try out, will he?"

"I will try to talk to him again." Mrs. Wu sat down on the bed next to Jade. Jade's bedroom was the only room in the house that looked completely Western. In the rest of the house Chinese design prevailed, with Chinese art and Chinese furniture. But Jade's room looked like that of any other teenage girl: posters of rock stars on the walls; teen magazines, books, and records heaped up everywhere. And she had decorated her bedroom just like one she had seen in *Ingenue* magazine.

Mrs. Wu stroked her daughter's hair. "Try to be patient with him. He's so proud of the world he comes from. He wants you to be, too."

Another tear rolled down Jade's cheek. How could she explain to her mother that she didn't share her father's desire to cling to the past? She wanted to be part of the world they were in now—Sweet Valley. And she wanted to be in the dance show more than anything in the world!

Jessica knocked on Elizabeth's door, and as usual opened it before Elizabeth answered. "Hi, can I come in?" she asked, barging in and throwing herself down on her sister's neatly made bed.

"Looks like you're in already," Elizabeth said wryly.

"Liz, what are we going to do about Dad? He's freaking out. I just found him downstairs in front of the mirror, counting the wrinkles on his face. He says he's going to throw out all his clothes and start dressing young. What are we going to do?" Jessica looked distraught. "What if he starts totally embarrassing us in front of all our friends? Or grows a mustache or something horrible?"

Elizabeth laughed. She thought her sister was exaggerating, as usual. "Well, we could just go along with it," she said. "I mean, sooner or later it'll pass, Jess. Let's not make a big thing out of it."

Jessica sat up, a devilish look on her face. "Liz, you're a genius," she said. "What a great idea!"

"What do you mean? What idea?" Elizabeth asked suspiciously.

"Suppose we go along with it—but I mean *really* go along with it. Convince Dad that being young is the greatest feeling in the world. We could drag him to the Beach Disco, play all kinds of hard rock for him, buy him trendy clothes. It ought to take about a week for Dad to realize he's better off being middle-aged—and young at heart—than trying to have some weird change of life-style."

Elizabeth laughed. "That might be kind of fun," she admitted. "You think it'll work in time for Dad's reunion?"

"Of course it will. Especially if we get Mom in on the act. She can take Dad to that new-wave nightclub downtown, where all those strange couples in their twenties hang out. He'll go back to being in his forties in no time!"

Elizabeth grinned. "I have to admit it's not a bad idea, Jess. But I don't think I can take any credit for it."

Jessica flipped her hair back and smiled. "I know. It was all my idea. So I'll have to take total credit for converting Dad back to a happy, well-adjusted middle-aged man once the scheme works. But right now I'd better go fill Mom in on it and make sure she thinks it's OK."

Elizabeth laughed. When Jessica decided to give an idea all she had, who could possibly get in her way?

Three

Tuesday morning Jade got to school early, hoping to find out more about the auditions before her first-period history class. But Ms. Bellasario was late, so unfortunately she didn't get the chance. And since Mr. Jaworski was strict about people being on time to class, Jade didn't want to ruin her perfect record by hanging around, waiting for the music teacher to show up. Besides, she was looking forward to seeing David again.

The first thing David did when he came into the room was look toward her desk. He flashed her a big smile, and she felt a nervous flutter in her stomach. He looked even cuter than he had the other day. *What's wrong with me?* Jade scolded herself. She had never felt anything like this before.

That week they were studying the Cultural Revolution in China. Jade was sitting in her usual place, behind Kevin Johnson, her notebook out in front of her. Usually she loved history. She was an extremely diligent student, though she didn't like to speak up in class. But doing this unit on China didn't appeal to her at all. She didn't like the looks the other students gave her, their expressions suggesting that she should be contributing something to the discussion, as if she knew more about the subject than they did. What could she tell them? Her father had left China before the Cultural Revolution, and anyway, she didn't like to be singled out. She wanted to be exactly like the other students. And now that she knew David was watching her, it made it all the more embarrassing.

To her relief Mr. Jaworski announced that he wanted to do something slightly different. But her heart fell when he went on to describe what that "something" was. "Instead of just talking about this one period in Chinese history, I thought we should think a little bit about Chinese culture at large. For example, what thoughts and feelings are prevalent in the East, and not in the West? It might help us to understand some of the events that took place in the last fifty years, and give us greater insight into the Chinese as a people."

Jade felt her face turn red. She couldn't wait until next week, when the unit on China would be finished and they would go back to studying European history.

Mr. Jaworski gave a short lecture about Buddhism. Then he showed some slides of Chinese temples and art. He ended with a short discussion about Chinese meals and other social customs. "But even here in America we've incorporated a number of Chinese customs. And there are a number of Chinese people living in our country who maintain old customs while taking up the new." He turned the lights on and shut off the slide projector. "Jade, what about your family? Do you still practice Chinese customs, or have you given them all up?"

Jade's cheeks flamed. She had dreaded this moment all week. All her classmates were turning around to stare at her, their expressions curious. They were looking at her as though she were a foreigner. That was the last thing she wanted.

"There's nothing unique or Chinese about my family," Jade lied, her cheeks still hot. "My dad doesn't run a laundry or anything."

Everyone in the class laughed.

Mr. Jaworski cleared his throat, looking upset and embarrassed. "Well," he said. "Uh, let's talk a little about one of China's close neighbors, Mongolia."

Jade fiddled with her pencil and stared at her notebook. She knew that she had been rude and that Mr. Jaworski only wanted her to contribute to the discussion. There were a number of useful things she could have said. She could have told the class about her mother's traditional costumes or the special Chinese meals they prepared. But instead she'd made a snide comment.

And the worst thing was that the stereotypical image she had made fun of—the Chinese laundry—was actually a part of her family. Her mother's parents ran a laundry right in Sweet Valley. One of Jade's deepest fears was that someone she knew would find out about it. Making it into a joke—making her classmates laugh about it—seemed to cover it up somehow, make it less likely that anyone would find out. Jade felt she would die if anyone knew. She loved her grandparents, but she couldn't help being ashamed of what they did. She was pretty sure nobody else's family was in the laundry business.

After class David hurried to catch up with her. "Was that true what you said in class?

Your parents don't keep up any of the old traditions?" he asked, looking almost disappointed.

Jade shrugged. "Not really. Why should they? They're American." She couldn't seem to keep herself from lying. What she told him was what she wished were true, with all her heart.

David shrugged. "I guess it's dumb to feel this way, but I think it would be cool to have an interesting family heritage like that. My family's so boring. Who wants to come from exactly the same background as everyone else around here? But yours—"

"Well, mine isn't too thrilling, either," Jade interrupted. She smiled to take the bite out of her words. She really liked David, and she didn't want him to get a bad impression.

But at the same time she couldn't see what was so interesting about being Chinese. If he *knew*—if he had any idea how restricting some of those traditional values could be—then he would understand why she wanted to keep it a secret.

The rest of the day wasn't any better. Jade forgot to meet Melanie after history, was late for all her classes, and couldn't seem to keep her mind on anything. "What's wrong with you? You seem a million miles away," Melanie complained at lunch. Jade just shrugged. She didn't want to tell Melanie that for the first time she was seriously considering doing something she knew her father disapproved of. She was so distracted, she was even late for her dance class that afternoon.

"This isn't like you, Jade. What happened?" Eve asked, clearly surprised.

Jade stripped off her street clothes to her leotard and hurried over to the barre. "Sorry, Eve. It's been a really tough week."

Eve looked at her closely. "Still worried about whether or not to audition for that school show?"

Jade nodded. "My father doesn't like the idea. I tried to talk to him about it last night, and he was just as negative as I expected. He said what I knew he'd say—that I can't do the show because it isn't 'serious' dancing. He just wants me to be the way women in his family have always been. I swear, he wishes we were still in China! He doesn't understand how I feel about dancing—it's my whole life!"

Eve patted Jade on the shoulder. "You know, one of the toughest things about growing up is realizing that you can have serious disagreements with people you love and still love them. You might have to help your father understand why this show is so important to you, Jade."

Jade stared at her. "You think I should go ahead and audition, don't you?"

Eve was quiet for a minute. "I think that you're very talented, Jade. And sooner or later you and your father are going to have to come to terms with the fact that your particular talent is one that needs a public. Dancers need an audience; it's part of the art. The sooner your father realizes that, the better it will be for both of you."

Jade nodded, her eyes fixed on her teacher's. "Eve, will you support me if I audition for the show? If it comes down to it, will you try to help me explain to my father exactly why this is so important?"

Putting her arm around the slim girl's shoulders, Eve said, "I promise to do everything I can to help, Jade. Because I think you're good enough. And I think you're ready to exhibit your talent, to show other people what you can do."

Jade felt her pulse quicken. She knew Eve was right. Dancing in the school show was just a small thing—and it was modern dancing, not the ballet she dreamed of performing in the future. But it would be her first opportunity to dance in front of an audience. And Jade knew she was ready. More than that, she *needed* to dance in front of people.

She just hoped she could come up with a way to make her father understand.

Jade had worked very hard during her practice session with Eve, and she was exhausted when she was through. Usually she walked home from her lesson, enjoying the chance to slowly unwind from the tough physical and mental demands of the ballet lesson. But that day she was just too tired. She decided to take the bus home.

To her surprise she ran into David Prentiss on the street outside the studio. He had his arms full of packages, and some of them were about to slide right out of his grasp. The uppermost one began to wobble dangerously.

"David, be careful!" Jade called out as she hurried over to help him balance the boxes.

"What are you doing with all these things?" she asked, after they had both caught their breath and the boxes were balanced again in David's arms.

David gestured with his chin at the delivery truck parked at the curb nearby. "I work part-time for a delivery service. Helps my mom with the mortgage." He grinned. "Can I give you a ride somewhere? I happen to be ahead of schedule this afternoon, so I can spare a quarter of an hour."

"Sure." Jade smiled at him. "That would be great. I was just on my way to the bus stop. Practice really wiped me out today." She watched him load the boxes into the back of the delivery van. Then he opened the door for her, and she scrambled up into the passenger seat.

"Have you always worked after school?" she asked him, as he got into the truck and put the key in the ignition. Most of the guys she knew seemed too self-absorbed to consider working to help their families out. Or else they were so well-off, they didn't have to think about things like money. She thought it showed a lot of maturity and responsibility on David's part. The more she learned about him, the more she liked him.

David nodded. "As long as I can remember. My dad took off when I was about seven. I've got five brothers and sisters, and we've all done what we can to pitch in and help. Even so, we're not in such great shape when it comes to finances. My mom works . . ." He looked briefly at Jade, as if he were trying to guess how she'd react to what he was about to say. "My mom works as a housekeeper. It's good money, but pretty hard work. So all of us do what we can to help out."

Now Jade was even more impressed. "Your family must be so close," she said. *Not like us,* she was thinking. *We can't even agree on the littlest things.*

David nodded. "I think we are. I'm lucky." He grinned as he backed the van out of the tight space. "Isn't that what families are for—pulling for each other?"

Jade swallowed. She thought about her own family, the tensions that had grown between them. She wished it could all be as simple as David made it sound.

"But anyway, enough of this heavy stuff," he said, seeming to guess her mood. "Tell me where you live, so I can take you home. And then tell me what you decided to do about auditions tomorrow afternoon."

Jade laughed. She gave him directions, then settled back, enjoying the view from the elevated vantage of the truck's seat. "I'm going to give it a shot," she said. Her hands felt sweaty, and she wiped them on her skirt. Until just then, when she'd said it, she wasn't sure she would have the guts to try out. But now she knew there was no turning back. She didn't know if she was glad or terrified.

"That's great!" David exclaimed. "I knew you would. Jade, I bet you anything you're going to get the solo dance part."

Jade blushed. "You really think so? I know lots of girls are trying out for it. A lot of them are older than I am. I've never even been in a school production before." Despite her years of dance lessons, Jade had never auditioned in front of a crowd. The very thought of it made her stomach turn over.

David slowed for a red light. "Listen," he said, regarding her solemnly. "I'll bet that you get the part. What do you want to bet?"

Jade smiled. "I don't like to bet. It's bad luck."

But there was no deterring David. "Well, I don't mind betting. Not when I know the outcome in advance. It's a funny thing, because I've never even seen you dance. But just watching you move—all your motions are so delicate, and at the same time you're so certain, like you know exactly what you're going to do. I've never seen anyone as graceful as you, Jade. I can't wait to watch your audition tomorrow."

Jade smiled deeply at him. "I'm glad you'll be there," she said quietly. "I think I'll dance my best, knowing you're watching."

She couldn't believe how bold she sounded. But it was so easy to be herself with David—to let him know exactly how she felt. And one thing was for certain: she was going to dance her very, very best the following afternoon. For Ms. Bellasario, for David, and for herself.

Four

Jade couldn't believe how nervous she was by the time four o'clock on Wednesday afternoon rolled around. She had called Eve to cancel class, explaining that she was auditioning, but Eve's pep talk made her all the more anxious. She wanted this part so badly! What if she didn't even get it, after the big deal she'd made?

"Look, you know I'll be there rooting for you," Melanie promised her. Jade didn't answer. She was thinking that that was part of the problem—knowing that so many people would be watching. Now she wished David wouldn't be there. What if she made some terrible mistake.

By the time Jade got to the auditorium, dozens of girls were crowded near the stage, giggling and gossiping about the show, about their chances of getting a part, and about who would be chosen as the solo dancer. Amy Sutton had a group around her—Cara, Jessica, Lila, and some other girls from the sorority—as she predicted her own success. "I've been working all week on my routine," she said loudly, tossing back her hair. "Look, I even got a new leotard for this audition."

Jade looked admiringly at the sparkling blue Lycra leotard. Everything about Amy Sutton made her seem like the perfect choice for the role of lead dancer. She looked like a model, with her blond hair and gray eyes. And she was so composed, so sure of herself, whereas Jade, even with her years of dance experience, trembled with nervousness.

Elizabeth Wakefield clambered up on stage and clapped her hands. "OK, guys," she called. "Ms. Bellasario is ready to start the auditions. Remember, the names of the acts chosen for the show will be posted first thing tomorrow in front of the office. OK? Ms. Bellasario will explain exactly how the audition will work."

A hush fell over the crowd as the music teacher strolled over to the stage. She crossed her arms and looked at the expectant group.

"First, let me remind you that we're auditioning musicians, vocalists, and dancers this afternoon. To make things easier we're going to take each group one at a time, starting with the dancers. Here's what we're going to do," she said. "Patty Gilbert, our student choreographer, will show you a combination, and you'll all do the same routine together. That will give us an opportunity to see the way you work in a team. Next we'll ask you to dance in small groups, five at a time. Then soloists will be asked back and will do their own combinations. Does everyone understand?"

There were murmurs of assent. Jade felt that fluttery sensation in her stomach that came when she was really tense. Her palms were damp, and her heart was pounding. She wanted the solo.

The first part of the audition went without a hitch. The girls formed several long lines, then the boys auditioned. Since there were fewer boys, they formed only one line. The assistant music teacher, Ms. Frankel, played the piano as Ms. Bellasario and Elizabeth took notes, watching from the first row of the auditorium.

"OK, fine. Now let's have small groups. First I'd like to see Jade Wu, Amy Sutton, Cara Walker, and Susan Stewart." Ms. Bellasario smiled at them.

Jade swallowed hard. She didn't know any of

the girls well, but she knew they were all juniors—and Amy and Cara were cheerleaders. Did that make them good dancers, too?

Amy Sutton was in a hurry to get onstage. "I'm halfway there," she whispered, giving the others the thumbs-up sign. "Did you guys see what Jessica wrote in my slam book? 'Amy Sutton, Best Dancer.' " She grinned. The slam books were something new at Sweet Valley High. Girls circulated them to write in their votes for outstanding class members. Jade felt her heart sink. Amy was sure to get the solo dance role. Upperclassmen were much more likely to get the big parts. Why delude herself?

The four girls lined up and waited for Patty Gilbert to come up on stage and show them the steps. To Jade the combination was simple—a series of steps, kicks, and light bounces. The others picked it up right away—all except Amy.

"I'm not ready," she complained. "There's something wrong with my shoe."

Everyone waited patiently while Amy fumbled with her shoe.

"OK, all set?" Elizabeth called.

"Wait a sec!" Amy called desperately. "I've got something stuck in my throat. I'm going to cough!"

Everyone waited for Amy to cough, but it seemed to be a false alarm.

43

"Now is everyone ready?" Elizabeth asked again.

"No, wait, wait a second. My hair's in my eyes. I need a rubber band," Amy cried.

Elizabeth was losing her patience. Jessica ran around the auditorium looking for a rubber band for Amy, and by the time she'd found one almost five more minutes had elapsed. "We're starting now, Amy, ready or not!" Elizabeth declared. She signaled to Ms. Frankel to begin playing the piano.

Then, when they finally began the routine, Amy's timing was off, and she practically ruined the whole group's rhythm. "I can't do this stupid thing," Jade heard her muttering.

"Thank you, girls," Ms. Bellasario said, clapping her hands together. "Now let's have the next group."

Amy was disgusted with her own performance, but rather than admit it, she turned to Jade, her eyes flashing with anger. "You threw me off, you know," she snapped. "Don't you know anything about dancing in a group?"

Jade couldn't believe her ears. She knew Amy had been the one who had almost thrown off the others. Even though Jade wasn't used to auditioning or dancing in a group, she knew her own steps had been flawless. But she was so in awe of Amy, one of the most popular juniors, that she could barely stammer out a word in her own defense.

"Amy," Cara objected, "it wasn't Jade. She—"

But there was no reasoning with Amy, who stomped off the stage and dropped into a seat beside Jessica.

Jade felt terrible. She quietly walked down the steps from the stage and took a seat in the tenth row. Jade watched as the other groups performed, and before she knew it, it was time for the solo auditions. David came over to where she was sitting and slid into the seat beside her. "I just wanted to say good luck," he murmured. "Will you stick around afterward so I can talk to you for a minute?"

Jade nodded. She smiled at him. Just knowing David was there was going to make all the difference.

Only six girls were called back to audition for the solo part: three seniors, Denise Hadley, Jennifer Morris, and Yvonne White; two juniors, Cara Walker and Susan Stewart; and one sophomore—Jade.

Amy was furious. "This is so unfair," she cried. And before anyone could say a word, she stormed out of the auditorium.

"Poor Amy," Cara said, "I'm glad I got a call back, but I feel bad for Amy. She really had her heart set on this.

Jade didn't say anything. She felt terrible about Amy's accusation that she had been responsible for throwing off her timing. Would Amy also blame her for the fact that she didn't get to audition for the solo part?

Denise went first. Her routine was simple but very well executed. Jade had to admit she'd danced very well. "I'm sure she's going to get it," she whispered sadly to David. "Look at how good she is!"

David scrunched up his face. "No way. You should've seen how you two looked together on stage. You're in a totally different league than she is, and it shows."

Jade felt so good, hearing David praise her like that! Up until now, she'd never heard praise from anyone but her dance teachers.

"Jade Wu," Ms. Bellasario called after Denise had finished her routine.

Jade stood up, her heart pounding. "Well, here goes nothing," she murmured.

David put his hand on hers. "Knock 'em dead," he said, smiling at her.

Jade climbed up on stage, gave her music to Ms. Frankel, then faced the group and waited until she had her concentration. Then, when the music began, she started her routine. She knew it was flawless, and when she was done, the auditorium seemed to explode with applause.

46

Elizabeth hurried over to tell Jade what a great job she had done, and Ms. Bellasario gave her a big smile as she shook her hand. "Nicely done, Jade," she said warmly.

"You were terrific! Absolutely terrific," David gushed when Jade sat back down next to him. "See, I told you you would be. I know you got the part, Jade."

"Don't jinx me," Jade chided him. "Susan hasn't even tried out yet. And Cara was really good."

But David was unshaken in his faith. "Nope, it's you, I know it. I know it," he said again.

For the rest of the audition Jade and David sat together. Gradually Jade felt her nervousness subside, and after Susan's audition, she actually began to relax and enjoy herself. When the singers and musicians were finished, Ms. Bellasario got up to thank the whole group and to remind them that the cast list would be posted the following morning.

"Phew," David said, getting to his feet. "That was completely draining. I think we'd better go out and get a hamburger at the Dairi Burger, don't you?"

Jade blushed. "I, uh, I can't. I have to go home and—" She broke off. *And what? Help my mother with dinner?* That sounded like a weak excuse—she was hardly going to say that. "I just can't," she said.

She couldn't tell David the truth: that she had been forbidden to go out on dates. Dates, according to her father, meant *any* planned activity alone with a boy. He probably wouldn't even have let Jade ride home with David the day before if he had known about it. And he'd certainly never allow her to go to the Dairi Burger with him.

David looked upset. "Well, maybe some other time," he said. She could tell from the look on his face that she had hurt his feelings.

But how could she explain to him that her parents wouldn't allow her to do things that other people simply took for granted?

"What did you guys decide?" Jessica demanded when her sister walked through the front door. "Do you realize Amy Sutton's called me four times this afternoon to ask if you were home yet? She's totally outraged about what happened. She wants to make sure Cara or Susan got the solo."

Elizabeth brushed past her sister and put her books down on the hall table. "Jess," she said patiently, "you know I can't tell you one single thing about the auditions. The list will be posted tomorrow morning, and Amy can find out the news when everyone else does."

48

Jessica looked closely at her. "OK," she said cheerfully. "But you can tell me, can't you? I promise I won't breathe a single solitary word to Amy. Cross my heart."

Elizabeth rolled her eyes. "You've got to be nuts. You'd tell Amy the second I told you. I might as well just call her and tell her myself. No, wild horses couldn't drag the information out of me. So quit giving me that wide-eyed innocent look of yours."

Jessica glared at her twin. "My own sister doesn't even trust me," she snapped. "That's nice."

Elizabeth laughed. "Come on, Jess, you know it's confidential—I can't tell anyone, not even you. Besides, we have to figure out what to do about Dad right now. Did you see that tie he wore to work this morning? I don't know where he got it, but it was purple, and it had all those weird paint swirls in it. I wouldn't let Jeffrey wear something that wild! Let's face it, he's going through this crisis in a big way."

Jessica followed Elizabeth into the kitchen and watched her take some cold chicken out of the refrigerator. "Well," Jessica said matter-of-factly, "I happen to have thought about it a lot today. I think the first stage of our scheme should be getting him to go with us to the Beach Disco on Friday night. I happen to know the Razors are playing. And you know what Dad thinks of rock music.''

Elizabeth laughed. ''It's a good idea, but I don't know if Dad'll fall for it, Jess. How in the world are we going to get him to the Beach Disco?''

''We'll figure something out. How about if we say you're going with Jeffrey, and I was supposed to go with A. J., but at the last minute he couldn't make it. So I'll tell Dad I can't possibly go alone. That might work.'' Jessica shrugged. ''And meanwhile, we just have to pretend we're taking him incredibly seriously. Like we know how he feels, worrying about his age, and we want to do everything we can to help him act younger.''

Elizabeth grinned. ''OK. Maybe dinner tonight is the time to start!''

''You should've seen me in my exercise class today,'' Mr. Wakefield said at dinner, sounding depressed. ''I must've been at least ten years older than anyone else there. I looked terrible. And I couldn't do any of the stuff the other men could.''

Mrs. Wakefield patted him lovingly on the arm. ''I think what you need is a change in life-style, honey. How can you possibly be in good shape if you spend eight hours a day sitting behind a desk? That's why I've enrolled you in this marathoners' club."

She handed him a brochure. "See? You start training gradually, and within a couple of months you're running twelve miles a day. That ought to make you shed a few years."

"Not to mention pounds," Jessica said helpfully.

Mr. Wakefield looked at his wife and then at his daughters. "You really think there's hope? That I can make myself younger by working out more?"

"Absolutely," Jessica said, beaming.

"Your exercise bike is due to be delivered tomorrow," Mrs. Wakefield said cheerfully. "An hour a day, along with your exercise class, and a jogging program, and you'll be in better shape than anyone else at that reunion."

She gave the twins a wink, and they grinned at each other. With the young life they planned to present to their father, there was no telling how quickly he would realize that middle age was the best thing going!

Five

As Amy Sutton turned away from the bulletin board near the principal's office, there was a look of complete disgust on her face. "I can't believe Ms. Bellasario is giving a *sophomore* the lead dance part in the show. It's totally unfair."

"You did a good job, Amy," Jessica said loyally, patting her on the shoulder. "Maybe Jade's just had more *practice* than you have." She didn't want to risk telling Amy that she thought she had done an awful job at the auditions and was lucky to have a part in the show at all. Amy was clearly upset and angry about getting a smaller part in the show—she was going to be dancing in the grand finale chorus line with all the others—and Jessica knew better than to bother Amy when she was upset.

"Hah, practice!" Amy snorted. "That's a total joke. It's just because she's got a dancer's body, that's all."

"What does that mean?" Jessica asked, trying to suppress a smile. When Amy Sutton was unreasonable, she could be very imaginative.

But Amy was watching Jade as she headed in the direction of the bulletin board. "Let's go," she said in a low voice. "I don't want to be here when she starts shrieking with joy. It's enough to make me sick."

Jessica shrugged. She thought Amy was being a bad sport, but when she considered how much her friend had wanted the coveted lead dance role, she wasn't all that surprised.

Jade couldn't believe her eyes. But there it was, right at the top of the list: Solo Dancer, Jade Wu.

"Didn't I tell you?" Melanie said, coming up behind Jade. She gave her friend an enthusiastic hug. "I want to take you somewhere great to celebrate. Why is it I have to go to geometry instead?"

Jade just smiled. She barely knew what she

murmured to Melanie as her friend turned away from the posted list to hurry off to class. She was too dazed. In fact, she barely noticed at first that David had come up behind her. She watched as his eyes scanned the list eagerly.

"You got it!" he cried, throwing his arms around her and giving her a hug.

Jade's heart began to pound. It felt like the most natural thing in the world, but she'd never been hugged by a boy before. In fact, she had never even held hands with a guy or been kissed. When David let go of her, she was blushing furiously.

She stared down at the ground, hoping her discomposure wouldn't show. She thought David was wonderful. She would never have believed that a guy could be as thrilled by her success as her friend Melanie was. David really seemed to care.

"The best thing is that I get to design the posters around you," David was saying excitedly. "What are you doing during lunch? I want to get started right away. I've got everything set up in the art room, I just need . . ." He looked deeply into her eyes. "Jade, you're such a beautiful girl. Do you have any idea how great it is to have a model with such distinctive features?"

Jade flinched at the word *distinctive*. *That*

means different, right? Not like everyone else, she thought.

She pulled away. "There's nothing special about my looks," she mumbled.

David was too caught up in his excitement about the poster design to notice Jade's discomfort. "I'd like to set it up in a way that uses some symbol of the show—maybe the chorus line—as the background, with you in the front, dancing."

Jade took a deep breath. She wondered how her father would feel if he saw a poster of his daughter. "Where will these—uh—be distributed?" she asked.

David shrugged. "I'm not sure. You'll have to ask Elizabeth, she's still in charge of publicity. I'm just supposed to capture the reason for the show—raising money for dance classes—and at the same time make the poster really special." He smiled. "And I think having you as a model will take care of that just fine."

Jade bit her lip. She didn't want to tell David, but she had a feeling her family wasn't going to like this poster.

And Jade couldn't help wondering whether she would like it, either. David had said something about her "distinctive features." Was he going to make her look ethnic? Jade worried. She was trying so hard to look just like everyone else!

"OK," David said. "Why don't we get started today at lunchtime? I'll take some photographs to work from, then sketch you, if that's okay with you."

Jade nodded. She liked how confident and happy David sounded when he talked about art. But at the same time she felt strangely shy. She had never posed for anyone before, let alone a boy she liked as much as she liked David.

It seemed as if the lunch hour arrived before Jade was ready for it. At David's request she had changed into the clothes she had with her—leotard, tights, and a dance skirt. She felt shy appearing in dance clothes in front of him, but he put her at ease with a warm smile.

She posed in various positions while David took an entire roll of film. Then he did a series of quick sketches, some portraits, others full-length. Neither of them said a word while he drew, and all Jade could hear was the sound of the pencil moving swiftly across big sheets of paper.

Finally David had a sketch that he thought he could work from to design the poster. "You see," he murmured when she came over to observe what he had drawn. "Your eyes are so beautiful, Jade. And your hair is finer than silk. I'll never be able to capture it exactly." He cleared his throat, a little embarrassed. "But anyway, the poster will be on a totally different scale. You'll be sketched in full against some kind of backdrop—probably against a scene that illustrates the importance of dance and music, to show what we're raising money for."

Jade looked curiously at the sketches. She felt incredibly shy, as she looked at his images of her. But she thought they were very good.

"I like them," she said softly, unable to look him in the eye.

She thought about her father. If he knew her image was being plastered all over the school as an advertising campaign for the show, he would be furious.

But the poster was part of the show. And Jade was determined to stay in it, no matter what.

Rehearsals for the show started that very afternoon. A dozen dancers had been selected—four boys and eight girls. Jade knew only one of them well, a sophomore named Betsy Weiss. The others were juniors and seniors. Amy Sutton, Susan Stewart, and Denise Hadley were sitting together in the auditorium, giggling and whispering. The Droids, Sweet Valley High's own rock group, were setting up their instruments for the song they were going to perform. A cluster of students chosen to do vocal acts was hanging around the stage. And then there were the set designers: David and his assistant, DeeDee Gordon, and two sophomores.

Holding a clipboard in her hand, Elizabeth Wakefield was talking to Ms. Bellasario when Jade walked up toward the front of the auditorium. Elizabeth put the clipboard down and came forward, smiling. "We're so glad you're going to be in the show, Jade," she said.

Jade smiled back. She only knew Elizabeth Wakefield and her twin sister from a distance, but she really admired them both. And from what she knew of them, Elizabeth was the one she guessed she would have most in common with. She would love to have Elizabeth as a friend.

"OK, everyone," Ms. Bellasario said, clapping her hands. "Let's all come up to the stage so that I can tell you how the show is going to work. Remember, we don't have that long to rehearse. The show is two weeks from tomorrow, on Friday night, and we have a lot to do before then." She opened a notebook and studied it for a minute.

"Now, the plan is to break the show into

three parts. First we'll have the musical acts. That includes The Droids' number, a couple of instrumentals, and all the singing. Then there will be a short intermission, and then we'll have our final dance acts: the scene from *The Nutcracker*, Jade's solo, and our grand finale chorus line." She gave Jade a big smile. "Jade, how long do you think you can dance? Is ten or fifteen minutes about the right length?"

Jade nodded. "That's perfect," she said. Actually, there was a routine she had been working on with Eve that lasted about that long—a modern dance number that was based on an old Chinese dance. It was a graceful, beautiful dance, and Jade hoped she would be able to use it in the show.

"Now, I need to introduce two very important people to you. First there's Elizabeth Wakefield. She'll be the one to come to with problems of any sort—before you come to me!" Ms. Bellasario pretended to growl, and everyone laughed. "Elizabeth is in charge of all sorts of administrative things. Getting tickets, doing some PR so we get a little attention outside of school, all that. So make sure you keep an eye on her."

Next she turned to David. "Now, this man is also essential to the show. David Prentiss will be in charge of sets and poster design. He's the guy who will make the show look right in every way. So be sure to get to know him and his assistants. OK?"

Everyone nodded.

"Now, if it's all right with you, I'd like to run rehearsals every single afternoon from four till six. How does that sound? When we get closer to show time, we'll have evening rehearsals, too."

Jade clenched her hands into fists and kept her head down so no one could see her face. Four till six! She always came home from dance class at five, to help her mother with dinner. There was no way she would be able to keep being in the show a secret. Obviously she was going to have to tell her mother. That meant her father would find out, too. Her mother would never be able to keep a secret from him. She would say it was wrong.

Jade wasn't worried about Eve—Eve would be overjoyed to let her take two weeks off from class for the chance to dance in public. But her father . . .

Jade just dreaded what was going to happen when she told him about the show.

Ms. Bellasario had finished her introduction, and the performers were milling around, introducing themselves and chatting before they dispersed. Real rehearsals wouldn't begin until the next day. Elizabeth came over and sat down next to Jade.

"I'm really looking forward to the dance you're going to perform," Elizabeth said with a smile. "Have you been dancing a long time?"

Jade nodded. "About six years. I've always wanted to dance, since . . . oh, since I can remember."

"Well, you're amazing to watch. There's something almost haunting about the way you dance." Elizabeth looked thoughtful. "I wish I could describe it better. But anyway, it's really wonderful to watch you."

Jade smiled. Everything that was happening seemed like a dream come true. Getting to be in the show, getting to know Elizabeth and some of the other girls. . . . Then she remembered to ask Elizabeth about the poster. "David told me you know where the posters will be hung up. Will there be any downtown?"

Elizabeth nodded. "Oh, sure. We've got to put up as many around as we can. We want to bring in a lot of money."

Jade's face fell. There was no way she could hide this from her parents.

Elizabeth saw the look on Jade's face. "I didn't say something wrong, did I?" she asked.

Jade slipped her book bag over one shoulder. "No, of course not," she said. It certainly wasn't

61

Elizabeth's fault! "I'll see you tomorrow at rehearsal," she said. At the same time she was thinking, *that is, if my parents even let me come back tomorrow.* She gave David a small wave as she strolled out of the auditorium. Her parents just had to let her keep the part in the show!

Jade waited until what she thought would be the best time to approach her father. They were eating dinner, and her father seemed to be in a good mood. He had been praised by his boss at work, and he seemed much more like himself than he had recently—cheerful, calm, good-natured.

"How was your day, Jade?" he asked.

Jade took a deep breath. "Great," she said. She smiled at him. "I have good news. I was chosen for the lead part in the show the school is putting on."

Mrs. Wu took a deep, sharp breath. Dr. Wu folded his napkin and stared at his daughter.

"I see. And what sort of show is it?"

"The dance and music show I was telling you about. I've been chosen to dance a solo." Jade could see he was getting angry. "Eve thinks I'm ready, Father. It's the break I've been waiting for. Please don't—"

"Absolutely not," Dr. Wu said. "Private ballet lessons are one thing. I'm not thrilled about it, but since your grandparents gave you the lessons as a present and since they don't seem to be doing you any harm, that's fair enough. But this isn't ballet, I take it. It's some kind of popular dance, like modern dance, right?"

Jade nodded, her eyes lowered.

"I simply won't allow you to disgrace yourself, Jade. In our culture dancing has a sacred significance. Your mother and I don't ask for much, but we do ask that you maintain enough pride and don't debase yourself and your heritage by making a public display of yourself in some so-called modern dance."

He paused for a moment, and Jade was tempted to run from the room. But before she could stand up, he went on. "I told your mother this would happen. I told her those lessons were a bad idea. My feeling was that you should stay home after school, help your mother, learn more about your own people and your own culture. I didn't see any point in these lessons. But your mother and your grandparents insisted you loved them so much that I gave in to your wish. Well, this time I will not. You are *not* to dance in public, Jade. Never!" And with that he threw down his napkin and stormed out of the room.

Mrs. Wu hurried over and hugged her daughter, stroking her hair gently. "Darling, he doesn't mean to be cruel. To him, it's a disgrace. He doesn't understand how important it is to you."

"Mother, I can't give it up. I just can't." Jade's face was wet with tears. "I really need to dance in this show. Can you understand that?"

Mrs. Wu nodded. "I think I do. We'll have to think of something." She sighed heavily, then said slowly, "Maybe if you keep going to the rehearsals, for now . . . we can keep it a secret from him until I talk him into it. . . ."

Jade wiped her tears away with a napkin. If her mother was on her side, maybe it would work out after all. "Oh, mother, thank you!" she cried, throwing her arms around her.

Mrs. Wu looked at the closed door of Dr. Wu's study. "But there's no way he can find out. Not yet," she murmured. "Jade, I don't know if I can convince him. And if I can't, you have to be prepared to quit the show, even if it's at the last minute."

Jade looked at her without saying a word. She couldn't imagine giving up the show. She had to believe that her mother would convince him. But at least she had her mother's permission to go back to rehearsal the next afternoon!

Six

"OK," Jessica whispered to Elizabeth. "Now, remember, A.J. suddenly got sick. So I'm going to try to get Dad to come to the disco with me, you, and Jeffrey." Actually, A.J., Jessica's new boyfriend, wasn't sick at all. He had gone out for the evening with his parents. But he had agreed to back up Jessica's story to help the twins in their keep-Dad-from-wanting-to-be-young scheme.

It was Friday night, and the twins were upstairs discussing strategy before going down to the living room, where their father was relaxing with the paper—his usual Friday evening custom. Mrs. Wakefield was reading a novel.

Elizabeth slipped downstairs, and her twin

followed right behind. Both were dressed to go out, Elizabeth in a pair of slim-cut black jeans and a silk top, and Jessica in a brand-new miniskirt and T-shirt.

"Hi, Dad," Elizabeth said nonchalantly. "You look kind of bored. Nothing on TV?"

"What?" Mr. Wakefield said, looking up with surprise from the paper. "Oh, no, I was just reading the paper leisurely—not the way I do all week, rushing to get through it before work."

Jessica frowned. "I don't know, Dad. Seems a little dull, just hanging out with the paper." She winked at her sister. "Hey!" she exclaimed, slapping her forehead as though a thought had just come to her. "Liz and I have been upstairs trying to figure out who I can get to come with me to the Beach Disco tonight. Liz is going with Jeffrey, and A.J. is sick and can't go. What about *you*, Daddy?"

Mr. Wakefield put the paper down and gave a little sigh that sounded as if he had been happier before they came downstairs. "You want *me* to come with you to the Beach Disco? Why?"

Jessica shrugged. "You might like it. There's this great band playing—brand-new music, Dad. Young music," she added pointedly.

Mrs. Wakefield tried to hide a smile. "What a nice idea, girls. Ned, doesn't that sound like fun?"

66

Mr. Wakefield grimaced. "I don't think I like brand-new music."

"Dad!" Jessica objected. "How do you know? You've never even heard it. Being young is an *outlook*. And if you want to feel young, you've got to be up on all the latest things, including the latest music." She tugged at his arm. "Besides, I don't have a date tonight. Come on, Dad. Come with us, please."

"The girls are right, Ned. You really should go," Mrs. Wakefield said.

Mr. Wakefield looked pained, but at last he took off his reading glasses and folded up the paper. "Oh, why not?" he said, beginning to smile. "After all, you're right about being young—it *is* an outlook. Why shouldn't I surprise myself and end up loving the Beach Disco?"

"That's right!" Mrs. Wakefield exclaimed, winking at the twins.

Elizabeth had to suppress a giggle as she watched her father get ready for the evening. He changed his shirt twice, rolled and unrolled his sleeves, and then asked their advice about his shoes. He modeled four different outfits before he came downstairs in what appeared to be his final choice: a pair of corduroy pants, a conservative striped shirt with the sleeves rolled up, and his new purple tie. After several reassurances from Jessica, he seemed satisfied that he looked young enough, and the twins dragged him out to the garage.

"Come on," Elizabeth urged. "We're meeting Jeffrey there in ten minutes."

Mr. Wakefield looked at the Fiat Spider the twins shared and then longingly at his own sedan, which was spacious and comfortable. "You don't really want to put all three of us in the Spider, do you?" he inquired.

"Daddy," Jessica protested, "the sedan is for old people. Come on—you can fit in the back." And with a grin at Elizabeth, she popped the front seat forward. The Fiat was really a two-seater, with a small space in back of the seats, where one person could sit—uncomfortably. But Mr. Wakefield was obviously determined to be a good sport. He looked completely mashed in the back, and Elizabeth felt a twinge of guilt. But then she remembered that this was all for a good cause.

"Are you OK back there, Dad?" she asked.

Mr. Wakefield cleared his throat. "I'm feeling younger by the minute," he said dryly. "I haven't ridden in a space this small since my fraternity days at college."

Twenty minutes later Jessica pulled into a parking space at the Beach Disco with a little squeal of the tires. "We're here, Daddy! Jump out!"

Mr. Wakefield surveyed the scene in front of

him with confusion. The Beach Disco was a popular weekend hangout, named for its position right on the water at the edge of town. It wasn't much more than a ramshackle old building with a dance floor, but it attracted a lot of new bands and had a reputation for being a fun place. That evening it was even more crowded than usual. Kids were everywhere—out on the beach, in the parking lot, and spilling out of the front entrance.

"This is going to be great, Dad," Elizabeth said. She tugged her father's arm gently when she saw him begin to hesitate by the car. "Come on, let's go in!"

The three of them made their way through the crowded entrance of the disco. Inside, the place was even more packed. The band Jessica had told Elizabeth about—the Razors—was up on stage, playing earsplitting heavy metal music. The dance floor was so crowded, no one could really move. Cigarette smoke had created a huge hazy cloud over the room, and the sound of laughter, music, and shouting was deafening.

"Isn't this great?" Jessica screeched at her father above the music.

Mr. Wakefield's hands flew to his ears. "What *is* this horrible noise?"

"Shh," Jessica hissed loudly. "Daddy, they happen to be very talented." She looked around her. "I'm sure a lot of their friends are here tonight. You wouldn't want to hurt their feelings, would you?"

"Heaven forbid," Mr. Wakefield said sarcastically. Just then both Jessica and Elizabeth spotted Jeffrey at a table over in the corner. They waved to him and tried to make their way through the crowd, with their father struggling along behind.

Jeffrey had been instructed to coach the group at the table to be especially loud when the twins and Mr. Wakefield arrived. Winston Egbert, the unofficial clown of the junior class, seemed eager to try his hand at making Mr. Wakefield's night miserable. The table was crowded with the twins' friends: Winston, Maria, Lila, Cara, Amy Sutton, and Ken Matthews.

"Mr. Wakefield! Nice to see you!" Winston cried.

"What did you say?" Mr. Wakefield cried back.

"I said, 'Nice to see you!' " Winston repeated, full volume.

"Daddy, sit down," Jessica instructed, pulling a chair out for him.

Mr. Wakefield looked around with an expression of combined misery and confusion. "You mean to tell me you kids come here and listen to this stuff on purpose?"

Jessica was staring at the band with a rapt look on her face. "This is my absolutely favorite song," she shrieked as the Razors broke into "You Tear Me Up." "Come on, Daddy, you just have to dance with me!"

Before Mr. Wakefield knew what was happening, Jessica had pulled him halfway across the crowded floor. There was no space for them to dance, but Jessica began to writhe to the music as her father stared at her in utter horror.

"Jessica!" he complained. "What on earth—"

"Exscuse me," Ken Matthews said, stepping on Mr. Wakefield's foot. He and Amy had followed Jessica out to the floor and were trying to dance as closely to them—and as rudely—as they possibly could.

"I don't think I've got the rhythm of this particular song," Mr. Wakefield said awkwardly, watching the dancers around him undulate to the music. "Jessica—"

"Come on, Daddy! This is fun!" Jessica cried.

Looking tired and pained, Mr. Wakefield wiped his brow. "I didn't think anything could be worse than exercise class, but this may change my mind," he yelled. "Jessica, let's go back and sit down," he said. "I think I need some club soda. It must be ninety-five degrees in here."

Jessica obligingly led her father back to the table. "I don't know if they have club soda here, Daddy. But they have wonderful grape-lime-raspberry fizzes. You should get one of those."

"That's OK," Mr. Wakefield said weakly. He stared bleakly around him at the jammed dance floor and shook his head. "Look," he said, "this is crazy. I'm going to call your mother and go home to my newspaper."

"Dad!" Jessica cried, trying to look hurt. "I thought you were sick of being middle-aged! Besides, if you don't stay, you won't hear the Razors' new hit—'Cut Me, Babe, Why Don't You Cut Me.' "

"What a shame," Mr. Wakefield said. "No, I'm going home." He squeezed her arm affectionately. "But thanks for including me." He shook his head as he pushed his way through the crowd to the telephone to call Mrs. Wakefield.

Jessica gave Elizabeth a triumphant glance. "Did you see how horrified he looked?" she cried with glee.

"He hated the music, that's for sure," Winston confirmed.

"Poor guy. I felt kind of sorry for him," Jeffrey said compassionately, putting his hand on Elizabeth's arm.

Elizabeth and Jessica burst out laughing. "It's all for a good cause, though," Elizabeth reminded him. "If he keeps having this lousy a time trying to be young, he's going to be the happiest person at his twenty-fifth high-school reunion!"

Monday morning at school David Prentiss announced that he had finished the poster for the variety show. A big group had gathered in the lounge at lunchtime, anxiously waiting for him to unveil it. Jessica was in the process of describing her weekend to a captive audience— Lila, Cara, Robin, and Maria. "We were torturing Daddy all weekend long," she said happily, as Elizabeth nodded in agreement. "The Beach Disco was just the first part of it. Then we decided he needed some really young clothes, so we took him to a men's boutique in the mall and made him try on some really trendy Italian stuff. He was so miserable! And then to really make things worse, his exercise bike got delivered. Our mom made him work out on it for two hours yesterday. He looked totally exhausted. I'll bet you he goes running to that reunion of his by the time we're through with him."

"Shh," Elizabeth said warningly. "David's coming."

Jade was sitting in the corner of the lounge, listening to the happy chatter around her with mixed emotions. She wished she could join in with everyone else, but she was really shy, and it was hard—even with a pretext like the show to talk about. She couldn't wait for David to come back from the art room with the poster. Embarrassing as it might be to see herself on it, at least David would be around. And she felt so much more comfortable when he was with her than when he wasn't. The truth was, Jade was really beginning to like David Prentiss.

The door to the lounge opened, and David came in, carrying a big cloth-wrapped rectangle. "OK!" he said, his eyes shining with excitement. "I'm ready to show you all the finished poster for Sweet Valley High's best ever show." He had brought an easel with him from the art room, and he set it up with a flourish. It took several minutes, but at last the easel was in place, and the covered poster was propped up on it.

"Ready?" David asked.

Everyone nodded. Jade felt her mouth go dry.

David slipped off the cloth, and everyone gasped. The poster was magnificent! David had sketched a chorus line in the background, with their arms linked. And superimposed over them David had painted Jade, bending down gracefully, arms lowered in a lovely dance posture.

"Oh, it's gorgeous!" Elizabeth said, admiring the way David had worked the lettering in on the bottom so the information about the show didn't obscure the central design.

David turned anxiously to Jade. "What do you think?" he asked.

Jade's eyes told him how she felt in her heart. "It's lovely, David. Really lovely," she said, her voice low and soft.

"I'm glad," he said. "Because I want to enlarge the center of this to use as a backdrop for your solo, if you'll let me."

Jade nodded speechlessly. She felt that her heart was too full to allow her to say another word. She saw something different in the poster than anyone else did: what she saw was how much David must care for her to portray her as being this beautiful.

Gradually everyone in the lounge dispersed, congratulating David and saying how much they liked the poster as they left. Not even the snide comment Amy made as she left could affect Jade's good mood. Soon only David and Jade remained in the lounge.

"David, the poster is gorgeous. I wish—" Jade was staring at him, a lump in her throat. "I wish I could tell you how much it means to me."

"You don't have to tell me. Just do me a favor."

Jade's face lit up. "Anything!" she cried.

"Let me take you out for dinner tonight after rehearsal," he said, putting his hand on her arm.

Jade swallowed. She turned away, not wanting to face him. What was she supposed to say now? That she wasn't allowed to date? That her father didn't even like her to talk to boys if they weren't Chinese? She couldn't tell David that!

Jade had a feeling that David had manufactured an idealized image of her—that she was something special, someone who stood out because of who she was and not what she was. She couldn't bear to tell him that she couldn't go out with him because her father forbid her to. So, instead, she stared down at the floor and mumbled another excuse.

"David, I can't. I've got all this stuff I have to do, and rehearsals are already taking so much time. This history homework—"

"Fine," David said, quickly picking up the poster and opening the door of the lounge to leave. "That's all right, Jade. I understand." But the bitterness in his voice betrayed how he really felt, and the look he gave her was full of hurt and anger.

Tearfully Jade watched David leave. It was dreadful having him misunderstand her. But she couldn't tell him the truth, either.

Monday afternoon was the first full-length rehearsal. Jade was going through her routine, a modern dance set to a Chinese melody which had been recorded—in a new arrangement—by an American jazz group. Jade had a cassette of the music playing as she rehearsed. Elizabeth slipped into a seat next to David. He had his head propped on his hands as he stared glumly up at the stage.

"Your poster is great, David. You really captured Jade's gracefulness perfectly," Elizabeth said.

David shrugged. "Yeah, I thought I understood her. But now I think I'm wrong," he said unhappily.

Elizabeth raised her eyebrows. "David, what's wrong? You seem really upset."

David turned to her. "Listen, Liz. Tell me the truth. If you were like Jade—real star material, with everything going for you—you wouldn't go out with someone like me, would you? Someone from a poor family whose mom works as a maid?"

Elizabeth stared at him. "David—" She didn't know what to say. "That wouldn't matter at all! And I'm sure it doesn't to Jade, either. She's not a snob."

David sank back in the chair. "I wouldn't have thought so, either, Liz. But if she isn't a snob, then why won't she go out with me? I've asked her a couple of times, and she keeps turning me down, giving me stupid excuses. I think she likes me—she sure acts like she does. But she won't go out with me." He paused for a moment. "I think she's ashamed to be seen with someone from a background like mine."

Elizabeth looked closely at David, her eyes full of compassion. "I'm sure you're wrong," she said, turning back to watch Jade execute a perfect dance step on stage. Jade was so beautiful, so graceful, yet so shy . . . how could she possibly be a snob? Elizabeth was sure there was no way Jade would spurn David just because his family didn't have a lot of money, or because his mother worked as a housekeeper.

But doubt nagged at Elizabeth, too. The truth was she didn't know Jade very well. She had noticed the sophomore didn't really seem all that open, or willing to share anything of herself. Was it possible David was right?

Seven

Jade couldn't believe how much being in the show changed her life. Rehearsals were held every afternoon for at least two hours, and everyone involved in the show started hanging around together at lunch and during study breaks. As Jade explained to Melanie, it was really important for the cast to get to know each other—especially the dancers who were performing together. "A show works so much better when we all give each other support and energy," she said, repeating what Ms. Bellasario had said at rehearsal on Wednesday.

In fact, Jade was quoting Ms. Bellasario quite a bit these days. Her mother kept warning her to tone it down, to try to suppress her excitement. Because as the days went on, there was still no sign of Dr. Wu changing his mind about letting Jade perform in the show. Jade was increasingly nervous about what was going to happen. Apart from her own disappointment if she had to quit, what would happen to the show if she dropped out? They didn't have another solo to replace her act, and the poster clearly billed her as the show's star.

"I don't see how you can stand it," Melanie commiserated as the two girls ate lunch together on Thursday for the first time in almost a week. "Isn't it hard to keep rehearsing when you don't even know if you can be in the show?"

Jade pushed her silky black hair back from her face. "If I thought about it, it would be hard. The truth is, I'm having so much fun rehearsing that I'm just trying to ignore the problem with my father. I guess I'm hoping some kind of miracle will happen, that my mother will convince him to let me go ahead." Jade sighed. "But the show's a week from tomorrow. I think at this point it *would* take a miracle."

What she couldn't express, not even to Melanie, was how hard it was becoming to lead a double life. No one else in the show had any idea that Jade's parents objected to her dancing.

They all treated her like a star—like someone who should do anything she could to advance her career. Despite the anxiety and guilt she felt about the possibility of having to quit, it was wonderful, for two hours a day, pretending. Jade came out of rehearsals feeling totally exhilarated, and it wasn't just from dancing in front of her classmates and hearing their praise.

For the first time in her life, Jade was spending time with a group of classmates in a way that seemed completely natural to her. She didn't feel awkward and shy. Instead, she was right in the center of things, and she felt as if she mattered. It was a wonderful feeling!

Besides, there was David. After she had turned him down for the date the day he'd unveiled the poster, things had been tense between them for the first few rehearsals. But that hadn't lasted, and the more time Jade spent with David, the more she liked him. He was honest, funny, warm-hearted—all in all, a great guy. The time they spent together, joking around or talking about the show, just flew by. She didn't want to give that up for anything.

"So what's going on between you and David Prentiss? You seem to be spending an awful lot of time with him lately," Melanie commented.

Jade took a sip of her soda. "I'm not sure,"

she said softly. "Sometimes I think . . . I don't know, that I might be kind of . . ."

"Interested?" Melanie suggested.

Jade blushed. "Mel, I just don't know. But you know the situation with my parents. They won't let me go out with anybody." She sighed. "Least of all someone who isn't a Chinese-American. I don't think there's much point in liking David, under the circumstances."

"Jade," Melanie said softly, "it might be time for you to stand up to your parents. Tell them what you really want."

Jade stared at her friend. Wasn't that the same thing Eve had said, though not in so many words? That she might have to show her father what mattered most to her? But Jade had a hard time imagining confronting her father about anything—especially about David Prentiss.

For now it was certainly true that nothing was going on between her and David. Sometimes she thought he liked her as more than a friend, but she wasn't ready to encourage him. And he was too shy to ask her out again without prompting.

As long as her parents felt the way they did, nothing could ever happen, not with David or any other boy.

Ms. Bellasario clapped her hands twice, a signal that the cast members should come up to the front of the auditorium for a brief meeting at the beginning of rehearsal.

"OK, everyone. Today is Thursday, which means we're only eight days away from show time. How's everyone feeling?"

Elizabeth laughed. "I think we're all pretty psyched, Ms. Bellasario."

Everyone else cheered, and Ms. Bellasario gave them a big smile. "Good. So far you're doing a fine job, and as long as you don't let your energy slack off, we should have a wonderful evening's entertainment on our hands a week from tomorrow." She glanced down at her clipboard. "We're scheduling two rehearsals this weekend, and we're probably going to want to start lengthening our rehearsals next week. In fact, you should all plan on working right through dinner some evenings. We can send out for pizza or something."

Jade bit her lip. How in the world was she going to manage that? It was hardly going to make her father more inclined to let her be in the show.

And it was becoming increasingly clear to Jade that there was no way she could drop out, not at this stage. What would happen to the others? They would never understand, and the show would be ruined for all of them. She had to find some way to convince her father to let her dance.

"One last piece of news before we get down to business," Ms. Bellasario continued. "I got a phone call today from a man named Mr. Wicker, a former dancer who now heads a prestigious troupe in Los Angeles. It turns out that he's interested in coming to watch our show—and for a very specific reason."

A hush fell over the group, and everyone listened attentively.

"Mr. Wicker told me that there's a wealthy woman named Amelia Higginson who wants to sponsor an internship for a talented young dancer who would perform with Mr. Wicker's summer stock dance company in L.A. This is an incredible opportunity, and Mr. Wicker intends to visit as many dance shows as he possibly can in search of the right candidate. He asked if he could watch our show next Friday night, and I told him we'd be honored."

David nudged Jade, his eyes sparkling with excitement. "Did you hear that? Jade, you're probably exactly who they're looking for!"

Jade swallowed. It was hard to believe her ears. A talent scout . . . coming to watch their show? And a chance of being selected for an internship with a summer dance company? It sounded too good to be true.

Trying to control the conflicting emotions she

84

was sure were visible on her face, she turned away from David. On the one hand she felt like he did: this was the chance of a lifetime. If Mr. Wicker came, and if she danced in front of him, she felt almost sure she could impress him and that she would have a real shot at the Higginson internship.

But an awful lot of *if*'s stood between her and that dream. First of all, Jade had to convince her father to let her dance in the show. Because if she didn't, Mr. Wicker would never even see her.

"You were really good today," David said after rehearsal. "I mean it. I bet if that guy Wicker was here watching you today, he'd have given you that Amelia Higginson award, no questions asked."

Rehearsal had just ended, and the cast was slowly dispersing. Jade slipped into her jacket. "You're just saying that," she replied.

"No way!" David said emphatically. "You know what I think about your dancing, Jade? I think you're going to go all the way to the top. And Wicker's going to spot your talent in a second."

Jade looked away. "Well, we'll see," she murmured.

She wished with all her heart that she could

confide in David. She wanted to tell him exactly how worried she was. But she couldn't. Everything depended on the confident all-American image she had tried so hard to build up. Here, among this group of people, Jade was looked upon as one of them. She wasn't going to burst that bubble by telling David about her cultural problems at home.

"Listen," David said. "I've got to make a delivery this afternoon, so I've got the van here. What do you say you let me take you out to celebrate your future career?" He grinned. "We could just get a sandwich and a soda somewhere." He saw her hesitate and added quickly, "I promise it won't be anything time-consuming because I know you've got tons of homework to catch up on and stuff. We could just go out for an hour or so." He glanced away, as if mustering his courage. "I want to take you somewhere, Jade. I want us to do something together."

Jade felt her heart ache. David was the sweetest, most forthright guy she had ever known. And she couldn't bear saying no again. But she knew her mother was waiting for her at home, and she had no choice.

She glanced anxiously at her watch. "David, I'd love to, but—"

David's smile quickly turned into a frown. "What is it, Jade? What bugs you about me?

Is it my background or something?" he interrupted.

"Your—" Jade started, then broke off. "Your *what?*"

"You know." David put his hands in his pockets and stared at the floor. He looked absolutely miserable. "My mom being a maid and stuff. And our not having much money."

Jade couldn't believe her ears. Was that what he thought? That she was ashamed of him because his mother worked as a housekeeper?

"David, you're out of your mind! Nothing in the whole world could be farther from the truth. No, it's just that I . . ." She faltered, not knowing what to say to make him feel better without revealing the real reason she couldn't go out with him. "I . . . well, there's just a lot of weird stuff at home. It's kind of hard to go into. It isn't anything to do with your mother or money or anything like that!" she protested, staring directly at him as she tried to think of something that might appease him.

But David still looked uncomfortable and embarrassed, as if he only half believed her.

"Listen," Jade said, lowering her voice. She put her hand on his arm and stared directly into his eyes. "Just to show you that there's no way that I'm that sort of person, I'll tell you the biggest secret I've got, OK? And once you know what it is, you'll realize how crazy you're being."

David looked at her.

"Guess what my grandparents do," Jade challenged him. "Go on—guess. I bet you'll never figure it out in a million years."

David shrugged. "I don't know. How would I know what they do? And what difference does it make, anyway?"

Jade took a deep breath. "OK, I'm going to tell you, but you have to swear on everything you can swear on that you won't tell a soul."

David shrugged his shoulders. "All right, I promise not to tell anyone." He was looking at Jade as if he didn't understand what she was making such a big deal out of.

"They run a laundry in Sweet Valley." Jade lowered her eyes and waited for his reaction, afraid of what it would be.

David stared at her. "So?"

"What do you mean, so?" Jade couldn't believe her ears. For as long as she could remember, she had been terrified someone would find out the truth about her grandparents. And now David was acting as though it didn't matter at all.

"I don't see what the big deal is," David said,

frowning at her. "Look, my mother's worked for years cleaning houses for people. Maybe it isn't the work she'd like to do most in the whole world, but it's supported the whole family since my father left. And to tell you the truth, I really respect her for it. I think she's fantastic. It sounds to me like your grandparents have done an awful lot for you, too. Aren't they the ones who pay for your dance lessons?"

Jade felt her face turn scarlet. "That isn't the point. They . . . well, it's just always made me feel funny, that's all. You know what all the stereotypes of Chinese people are like. It kills me, thinking that someone from school might find out one day . . ."

David shook his head. "I don't know what your grandparents are like, but to me what matters is who people are, not what they do. I really can't see what you're making such a big thing out of, Jade."

Jade was confused. She must not be making herself clear, she thought. It mattered so much that David understood how she felt about this. Her grandparents' laundry was the deepest secret she had—she had never told anyone about it before. And now David was acting as if she had no reason to worry about it.

"I still don't understand what any of this has to do with our going out," David added, his face set. "Jade, you haven't explained to me why we can't go out together. Unless you just don't want to."

"No—that isn't it!" Jade cried. If only there was some way to let David know how she felt.

"Well, I think that must be it," he added. "Because if you really wanted to, Jade, you would." And with a last unhappy look, he turned and walked down the hallway away from her.

Jade watched him go as tears filled her eyes. She couldn't believe what a mess she was making out of everything. She probably should have just told him the truth.

But how could she tell him that? He hadn't understood about her grandparents, and he probably wouldn't understand about her father and his beliefs, either.

Jade felt terrible. She liked David more than she had ever liked a boy, and she cared so much about his opinion. Why hadn't he understood how embarrassed she was about her grandparents' laundry? He had acted as though there was something wrong with *her*, not with them.

Not that Jade didn't love her grandparents, but she couldn't help feeling ashamed of what they did.

If only she could be like everyone else, she thought. There were two things she wanted more than anything in the world: to dance in the show in front of Mr. Wicker and to go out with David. And it looked less and less likely that either was going to happen.

Eight

Amy Sutton had been in a bad mood ever since Jade got the solo part in the variety show. She still couldn't believe Ms. Bellasario had made such a serious casting mistake, and the more she thought about it, the more it bothered her. It was bad enough going to rehearsal day after day when all she got to do was dance in a chorus line. But having to watch Jade get all the attention . . . it was almost unbearable! The poster David had designed for Jade was hanging all over school, so everywhere Amy turned she was reminded that Jade was the star. To make things even worse, at Saturday morning's rehearsal David unveiled the center set, which he had been working on all week. It was a huge blowup of one of the posters, with slight changes made so that Jade's graceful form stood out even more. Amy covered her eyes. "Not again," she groaned to Lila. "I don't think I can stand this any more!"

"What you have, Amy, is a bad case of jealousy," Lila said judiciously. Lila wasn't in the show, and so she didn't feel one bit competitive with the sophomore sensation. In fact, she seemed to be enjoying Amy's jealousy.

But that was only part of what Amy was feeling. She was also irritated by Jade's behavior. The way Amy saw it, Jade was taking advantage of being the "star." She was acting like a real prima donna, insisting on having water up on stage in case she got thirsty when she worked out, for instance. And she always left rehearsal at exactly five o'clock, whether they were through or not. Today, on her way to rehearsal, Amy had overheard Melanie Forman calling Jade a star. And that really bothered her. It was bad enough having a tiny, insignificant little part in the show. But watching Jade was driving her crazy! *Next thing we know she'll be demanding her own dressing room*, Amy thought crossly.

Rehearsal was only half over, and Amy was glad she had made plans to leave early and go shopping with her mother. She couldn't stand watching Jade a minute longer.

"I'm taking off," Amy told Lila. "Don't tell Bellasario—she'll never even notice I'm gone." And with that she slipped out of the darkened auditorium, glowering at the image up on stage of Jade, who was dancing in front of that marvelous backdrop.

Mrs. Sutton was waiting for Amy outside in the family car, a beige sedan. "Listen, I have to do one or two errands before we go to the mall. I didn't have time to take care of them before I picked you up."

Amy slouched down in the front seat. First she had to endure watching Jade Wu rehearse, and now she had to drive all over Sweet Valley with her mother doing errands. What a rotten Saturday this was turning out to be!

Mrs. Sutton glanced at her watch. "I've got to pick up some of Dad's shirts here," she said, pulling into a parking space at Sung's Laundry.

Amy frowned. "Why here? I thought you went to that laundry near the TV station." Amy's mother was a sportscaster at one of the local networks.

Mrs. Sutton shrugged. "I felt like changing, that's all. I like this place better now." She smiled. "You coming with me or staying in the car?"

"Oh, I guess I'll come in," Amy said dramatically, with a sigh that signaled how big a sacrifice she was making.

There were a few people ahead of them, and while they were waiting, Amy looked around the small laundry for something to distract her. Suddenly her eyes landed on a poster on the wall next to the cash register. It was the poster advertising the show at school.

"Hey, Mom!" she exclaimed. "That's the show I'm going to be in next week."

An elderly Chinese woman was sorting through laundry packages, and she turned to Amy with a smile. "My granddaughter will also be in that show," she remarked. "As a matter of fact," she said, pointing to the poster, "that is a painting of her."

Amy couldn't believe it. "Are you Jade Wu's grandmother?" she asked as politely as she could.

"Yes, I am. I am her mother's mother," the woman said proudly. "Do you know Jade well? Are you two friends? I can tell her we met."

"No—I mean, we don't really know each other very well," Amy mumbled quickly. "We're in different years. She's a sophomore. I'm a junior. I just met her at the auditions, actually." The whole time Amy was talking she was thinking, *Wait till I tell everyone at school! The snobby star of the show is really just the granddaughter of someone who runs a Chinese laundry!*

"I can't believe it," Amy sang out when she

and her mother left and got back in the car. "That's Jade's grandmother!"

Mrs. Sutton raised her eyebrows. "Is that such a big surprise? This isn't a huge town, Amy. Why shouldn't people be related sometimes?"

Amy shook her head. "You don't understand, Mom. Jade's the star of the show we're doing."

"So?" Mrs. Sutton said, putting the shirts on the backseat. "I still don't get it, Amy."

Amy rolled her eyes in exasperation. There was no sense in trying to explain something this important to her mother, who would never get the point.

But she knew the girls at school would immediately see why it was so funny. And it would make Jade look so ridiculous, after she had been acting like such a *star*.

Amy could hardly wait to get home and call Lila.

Jade woke up early Sunday morning. The sun was streaming through her bedroom window, and she sighed luxuriously. It looked as though it was going to be a beautiful day, and she was really starting to get excited about the show. The day before, when she came back from rehearsal, her mother had whispered, "I think your father is starting to thaw a little."

Jade didn't know exactly what that meant, but it was the first promising sign yet!

And today she had another rehearsal to look forward to. Only five days left till show time, and as Ms. Bellasario said, they needed every minute of rehearsal between now and then that they could grab. And after rehearsal, Jade hoped to get a chance to talk to David again.

Since their talk the other day, things had been cool between them again, which worried Jade. But she hoped that would go away. They still sat together during rehearsals, and they were starting to get teased by the other students. Everyone kept telling Jade how much David liked her. In fact, Melanie had called the night before to ask if Jade and David were "getting serious." Jade had laughed. How could they get serious, she countered, when she wasn't even allowed to go out on a date with him?

Maybe today they could take a walk, she mused to herself as she clambered out of bed. She felt mixed up when she imagined being alone with him. Part of her really wanted to be with him, but at the same time she was almost afraid to admit she had feelings for him.

Jade was feeling optimistic when she arrived at school later that morning for rehearsal. It was a funny feeling, showing up at school on a Sunday.

She was locking her bicycle to the rack in

front when Lila and Amy walked by. They eyed her curiously.

"Hey, Jade, I didn't know your family ran a laundry," Lila said casually.

Jade felt all the color drain from her face. "What?" she asked. She didn't think she could possibly have heard right.

"She said, she didn't know your family ran a laundry," Amy said cheerfully.

Jade struggled to maintain her composure. Before she knew what she was saying, the words flew out. "They don't."

"They don't?" Amy repeated tauntingly. She looked at Lila, and they both started to giggle. "Are you sure, Jade? What about Sung's Laundry, downtown?" And before Jade could respond, Amy and Lila flounced off, still giggling.

Jade's mouth dropped open. She felt as if she had been slapped in the face. How on earth had they found out about the laundry? Unless . . .

But David wouldn't have told anyone. Would he? After she'd told him it was a secret?

Jade felt terrible. The thought of walking into the auditorium and going ahead with the rehearsal made her sick. For the first time since moving to Sweet Valley she had felt good about herself. And now that was all over. Lila and Amy would spread the news in a matter of minutes. And everyone would know—not just that her grandparents ran a laundry, but that she had been ashamed enough to try to lie about it. "God," she moaned, slapping herself on the forehead, "what an idiot I am!"

Just then David raced up on his bike. Jumping off, he gave Jade a big smile. "Hi, how're you doing?"

"Terrible," she snapped. "No thanks to you, David!"

David stared at her, his happy expression fading as he fumbled with his bike lock. "What's wrong with you?" he managed to ask her.

Jade put her hands on her hips and glared at David. "What's wrong with me is that I don't happen to appreciate you breaking a confidence, that's what. When I told you that stuff about my grandparents running the laundry, it was completely private. And you told me you wouldn't say a word to anybody!"

"Yeah, and I didn't." Having locked his bike, David stood up and stared back at her. "Why would I? To tell you the truth, Jade, I didn't see what the big deal was then, and I don't now. Who cares what your grandparents do? But I made a promise, and I haven't said a word about it." He looked disgusted. "Who would I tell that to anyway? I can't think of a single person who would care."

"Yeah, right. Then how come Amy Sutton and Lila just *happen* to have found out? I suppose some little bird mentioned it to them? Just a few days after I told you?"

David's eyes sparkled with anger. "Look, Jade, either you trust me or you don't. I swear that I didn't tell a single soul your little secret, ridiculous as I think it is."

"It's not ridiculous!" Jade shrieked. "David, you're just the most insensitive, most—"

David broke in, his own voice getting louder. "Who's insensitive? You're the one who's ashamed of your own family, just because they do some kind of work that you feel is beneath you!" He stared at her indignantly. "I didn't have the guts to say this the other day, but I'll say it now. I think keeping your grandparents' job a secret shows there's something wrong with your attitude, Jade. And *that's* the real problem."

"Thank you very much, but I don't need you to tell me what my problem is," Jade said coldly. "Right *now* my problem is that somehow the whole school's found out about my grandparents, and I'd like to know how."

David walked past her. "I couldn't care less how anyone found out. I want to know why you can't face up to who you are, Jade. You know, until you do, you're going to have nothing but problems!"

Jade felt her eyes fill with tears. She reached out her hand to grab David's arm, but there was no stopping him.

"David, where are you going?" she cried. "Wait till we finish talking at least!"

But David had stormed inside the school. Jade followed him. She had never seen anyone this angry before.

"I'm through with this whole stupid show," he said, not turning around to face Jade but walking ahead of her, straight down the hall toward the auditorium. "I don't know what it means to you, but to me, it's all turned into something fake. I wanted to do all this stuff—like the posters and the sets—for you, Jade. Because I admired you so much. What a laugh! Now I just want out of the whole thing."

Silently Jade walked behind David. He opened the auditorium door with a bang and strode down the aisle and up on the stage. To her utter horror, David grabbed the central set, and ripped it down. Before anyone could stop him, he had charged out of the auditorium, leaving everyone staring at him.

It took every ounce of self-control Jade had not to break down and start sobbing right then. She was so upset that she felt almost dizzy. *Stay cool*, she instructed herself. She remembered what her father always said. *However upset you are, just keep your head. Don't break down.* But it was incredibly hard to follow his advice right now. Everyone was crowding around her, asking what was wrong with David, why he was acting that way, and if they had had a fight.

Jade just kept shaking her head, saying she didn't know. She couldn't bear to face the truth—that David had really and truly quit. That their friendship—and any chance of something more than that—was completely gone.

She couldn't ever remember feeling so terrible. The urge to run out of the auditorium after David and never come back was incredibly strong. *A dancer never runs out on a show*, Jade reminded herself, thinking of Eve. Never.

Everywhere Jade turned she felt as if people were whispering about her. She knew Lila and Amy would have told the whole cast about her grandparents by now. By tomorrow it would be all over school.

Everything had fallen apart, and Jade could barely force herself to go through the motions in rehearsal. In fact, she couldn't see much point in trying to go on with the show. Now that she had been exposed for what she was . . . now that David was gone . . .

For the first time, Jade made a series of mistakes when she went through her routine. She was so anxious and unhappy, she even fell once, and for a split second she was afraid she wouldn't be able to get up.

"Jade? Are you all right?" Ms. Bellasario asked with concern, hurrying over to the stage.

"I'm fine," Jade said dully, struggling to her feet.

But it wasn't true. She wasn't fine at all.

All the joy in the show was gone for Jade. She didn't even feel like dancing anymore. It was as if everything wonderful in her whole life had disappeared in a matter of minutes.

Nine

"OK," Jessica said, hurrying into Elizabeth's room without knocking. "It's time for Operation Middle Age, Liz. What are you doing just lying around in here when I need help convincing Dad that middle age is the best thing that ever happened to him?"

Elizabeth groaned. "I happen to be trying to do some homework, Jess." Frowning, she tossed her notebook down. "Boy, I'll tell you one thing about this show. It's sure taking a ton of time! We had rehearsal yesterday and rehearsal today. It feels like I never left school, and tomorrow it's going to be Monday again." She sighed. "I just hope it's worth it and the show is a smash on Friday night."

Jessica wrinkled her nose. "I'm sick of hearing about that show. It's all anyone talks about anymore. You should've heard Lila and Amy going on and on about it last night."

"What were they saying?"

Jessica shrugged. "I don't know. Amy was all bent out of shape because she found out Jade's grandparents own a laundry in Sweet Valley. So she's been running around having typical Amy-type fits about it, telling everyone what she thinks."

"That girl really knows how to gossip. What business is it of hers what Jade's grandparents do?" Elizabeth asked, outraged.

Jessica shook her head. "I don't know. Amy thinks it's obnoxious that Jade's pretending to be so high-and-mighty and everything when she's really not."

"Amy's impossible! Jade hasn't been acting high-and-mighty. Amy's just angry because Jade got the part she wanted. And Amy can't even dance—not very well, anyway."

"All right already!" Jessica said impatiently. "I came in here to talk to you about Dad, not Amy and that boring show. Don't you think—"

But Elizabeth cut her off. "Wait a minute, Jess. I do need to talk about the show for a minute. This whole thing with Amy is really beginning to worry me," she said. "I'm concerned about Jade. I know she's been under a lot of pressure, and I get this feeling that there's something bothering her. She's been really distraught at rehearsals lately. Amy gossiping about her family is only going to make things worse. I just hope Jade's going to be able to hold up under all the pressure."

Jessica shook her head. "Oh, she'll be all right. Stars are used to pressure, Liz. She'll do just fine."

Elizabeth shoved her books aside. "I wish Amy would mind her own business. She ought to know better."

"You're always complaining about Amy. She's perfectly justified, Liz, if she happens to want to talk about Jade," Jessica said, defending her friend.

Elizabeth was about to disagree when Jessica returned to the original topic of conversation. "I really want to talk about Dad, Liz. I think our plan is working. Have you noticed how upset he gets whenever I turn on the progressive rock radio station? And did you see the look on his face when we gave him that T-shirt from the mall yesterday? We have to be sure, though. I think he's ready for a middle-aged test. And I need your help to do it."

"What do you want me to do?" Elizabeth asked, looking at the pile of homework she still had to get through.

"Come downstairs with me. I want to see

how he reacts when I ask him to watch music videos with me."

Elizabeth groaned. "Can't you do that by yourself? Jess, I really want to get some work done."

Jessica sniffed. "Fine. If you don't care enough about your own father's middle-aged crisis, it's all right with me. I'll just have to check it out myself."

Elizabeth sighed. "OK, OK, I'm coming." She glanced at her watch. It was getting late, and she really did have a lot of homework to do. Also, she was thinking of giving Jade a call later on, just to see how she was doing. She was worried by what Jessica had told her about Amy Sutton and Lila Fowler. When those two made up their minds to make someone unhappy, there was no limit to what they would do!

Jade opened the door and walked into the kitchen, her head down. She had been out walking for hours since rehearsal ended, trying to clear her head. But she was still very distraught.

"Jade? I've been waiting for you," Mrs. Wu said quietly. She was taking things out of the refrigerator for dinner. "Are you upset about something?"

Jade nodded. She felt a rush of affection for her mother, who could always tell when something was wrong.

Jade blinked back tears. "Yes, Mother. Actually, there's been . . ." She stopped. How could she start explaining everything that had gone wrong? She couldn't tell her mother about David. It would only create more problems. "Something went wrong at school. It's kind of complicated."

"I'd like to hear about it," Mrs. Wu said, putting her hand on Jade's shoulder and giving her an affectionate squeeze. "You know I'd like to help if I can."

Jade sighed. "Well, some girls at school found out about Grandma and Grandpa's laundry," she said sadly. "I tried to keep it a secret, but somehow they found out. I felt so embarrassed, Mother, like it was all the stereotypes about Chinese people rolled into one."

Mrs. Wu didn't say anything. Then she pulled her arm away and went back to the refrigerator, pretending to look for something.

"I'm so upset," Jade continued. "Maybe it's wrong, but I just wish they didn't know. What do you think?"

When Jade's mother answered, her voice was full of anger and hurt. "I think your shame is in the wrong place. You have no business being ashamed of what Grandma and Grandpa do. They've always been wonderful to us. I happen to be very proud of them, and I think you should be, too."

Mrs. Wu's normally controlled voice shook

with emotion. "Listen," Mrs. Wu said. "My parents were both born in China. To come to this country took extraordinary effort for them, but they made it. They met here, you know that. You also know what self-sacrificing, selfless, loving people they are. They spent the best years of their lives giving and giving to my sisters and me. We had the best they could afford, always, even if it meant they went without." She sniffed. "That laundry supported us all for years. And I don't think I need to remind you of everything that Grandma and Grandpa have given you. For instance, those dance lessons."

Jade felt her face flame crimson. *That's just what David said,* she thought.

She hung her head while her mother continued. "I've tried very hard to stick up for you, Jade, whenever you've asked to do something that your father forbids. For years I've taken your side because I know how important it is for you to fit in with and to be like others. But I think you should show more respect for your own heritage. To be ashamed of your own family—" She frowned. "It's that attitude you should be ashamed of, not your grandparents."

Jade felt tears stinging her eyes. "Mother—"

Mrs. Wu wasn't through yet. "I have spent the greater part of the week begging your father to change his mind about this show. But how can I talk to him in good conscience, persuade him that this is what's best for you, when I see this kind of behavior? It's one thing to want to fit in, Jade, and it's altogether another to want to erase your identity, to deny your heritage. I simply won't allow it."

Jade didn't know what to say. Suddenly she felt deeply ashamed of herself. All the kind things her grandparents had done for her flashed through her mind. And she suddenly sensed that her judgment had been wrong in more ways than one. Why had she always been so ashamed of her own heritage? Wasn't that every bit as wrong as clinging to it too strongly, as she felt her father did?

"Mother," she said finally, "will you excuse me for a while before dinner so I can be alone?"

Mrs. Wu nodded, her face grave. "Please give what I've said some thought. I will not talk to your father until I'm satisfied that this show is really good for you. That it isn't corrupting you, making you ashamed of your own people and the person you really are."

Jade didn't answer. She knew her mother was right. She had a lot of thinking to do, and she wanted to be alone.

"Jade?" Mrs. Wu knocked lightly on the closed door of Jade's bedroom. It was late Sunday evening, and Jade had spent a long time lying on her bed, deep in thought.

"Yes, Mom?"

"It's the telephone, for you. A girl named Elizabeth Wakefield."

Jade thanked her mother and came out to pick up the telephone. "Hi, Liz. What's up?"

"Hi, Jade. How are you?" Elizabeth's question sounded slightly anxious. "I just wanted to talk to you about the show. You've been working so hard lately, and I wanted to find out how you're feeling about everything. I know how tense it can be when you're trying to balance schoolwork and a show and everything."

Jade bit her lip. "Actually—"

"What?" Elizabeth prompted her.

"Well, things *have* been kind of tense," Jade admitted. "I was—well, it's kind of dumb. I'm really upset about David quitting."

"So am I," Elizabeth said. "In fact, that's really what I wanted to talk to you about. Do you have any idea why he went storming off today?"

"We got in a big fight," Jade admitted. "I told David something in secret and he—well, he ended up blabbing it all over the place. I was really mad at him, and I let him have it. So I guess he got mad in return, and he ended up quitting."

Elizabeth was quiet for a minute. "That thing

you told him in private," she said thoughtfully. "Can I ask you what it was?"

Jade twisted the phone cord between her fingers. "Something about my family. About my grandparents," she murmured. "I really trusted David, and then he went ahead and told someone about it. So I got furious. Wouldn't you have?"

"You're kidding!" Elizabeth exclaimed, sounding happier. "You mean you got so mad because you thought David told people about your grandparents and the laundry?"

"I know he told them. How else would anyone have found out?" Jade asked.

"Amy Sutton," Elizabeth told her. "Apparently she and her mom picked something up from their laundry Saturday morning. She found out from your grandmother, and you know Amy. Or, if you don't, you do now. She's not exactly the best secret-keeper in the world."

Jade couldn't believe her ears. "How do you know it was Amy who told everyone?"

"Because Amy told my sister, Jessica, that's how." Elizabeth paused. "Is that the whole reason you and David got in a fight?"

Jade wanted to get off the phone in a hurry. "Yes," she said. "The whole reason."

She and Elizabeth talked for a minute or two more, but Jade was eager to get off the phone and quickly found an excuse to say goodbye and hang up.

She couldn't believe what an idiot she'd been, leaping to conclusions that way about David. Why hadn't she taken his word for it when he said that he hadn't revealed her secret?

Instead, she had accused him of all sorts of terrible things. After all the kindness he had shown her, it seemed inexcusable. She was ashamed of herself, really and truly ashamed.

And that wasn't the only thing that Jade was ashamed of. She had been doing a lot of thinking, about what her mother had said and about her attitude toward her grandparents.

She now realized that her mother was right, and so was David. Jade felt a quiver of embarrassment every time she thought about the way she had reacted—or rather overreacted—to anyone learning about her grandparents' laundry. Her mother's point seemed perfectly valid to her now. What difference did it make what they did? Her grandparents were the most wonderful, loving people, and they had always done anything they could for her, given her everything they could. When she thought of how hard they worked, and how good and kind they were to her, she felt overwhelmed with gratitude. She couldn't believe how rotten she had been to act as if their identity was something that had to be concealed.

And as for David . . . well, again Jade felt terrible. He'd been a real friend to her, and instead of giving him the benefit of the doubt she'd gone into a suspicious frenzy, accusing him of betraying her.

Jade took a deep breath. She wanted to make it up to him. Should she call him at home and tell him how sorry she was? She had her hand on the telephone, ready to call him, but she stopped herself. She had never called a boy before. And trying to explain something so personal on the phone just didn't seem right. . . .

No, she'd better wait until Monday, she decided. She would find him in school, first thing, and tell him how sorry she was. Hopefully he would join the show again, and life could go back to normal—only better!

Jade tiptoed down the hall to her parents' room, where she knew her mother would be getting ready for her bath. Sunday evenings her father always relaxed with the newspaper downstairs, so she was sure her mother would be alone.

"Mom?" she called softly.

Mrs. Wu was sitting on the edge of her bed, brushing her long silky hair. She smiled when she saw her daughter, but there was something guarded and tentative in her expression that Jade had never seen before.

"Mom, I want to apologize about what I said. About Grandma and Grandpa. I was really a jerk," Jade said. She took a deep breath. "I can't believe I was making such a big deal out of nothing."

Mrs. Wu smiled at her. "You worried me," she said gently. "I didn't want to see that kind of attitude—least of all in you, Jade. Especially knowing how proud they are of you, loving you the way they do."

Jade nodded. "Mom, please forgive me." She took a deep breath. "I'll understand if you feel you can't talk to Dad about the show."

But her mother shook her head. "No, darling, I know how much it means to you. And I promise to try. From the way he sounded last night, I think he may be willing to reconsider." She sighed. "As long as you don't forget who you are, Jade. And who we are."

Tears of relief filled Jade's eyes. "I promise I won't," she said.

Mrs. Wu stood up and hugged her daughter tightly. She still had to apologize to David, and she had no idea if he would even listen to her after the way she had treated him. She could only hope so.

Ten

Jade could hardly wait to get to school Monday morning. But as it turned out, she couldn't find David anywhere before their first-period history class. And David came into the classroom so late that there was no chance to talk.

As he walked past her to his desk Jade started to say, "David—"

But he turned away, and Mr. Jaworski asked everyone to sit down so class could get started. Jade watched David sit down, dismayed by his cold reaction. He wouldn't even look at her!

After class she cornered him at his desk. "David, I really need to talk to you. Please?" she asked, her voice desperate.

David shifted his weight from one foot to the other. "I've got a lot of stuff to do. And I have a lot of things on my mind," he muttered. "Maybe later, Jade."

"It's about what happened yesterday, and about the show. Please, David, it's really important."

David ran his hands through his hair. He looked pale and exhausted. "To tell you the truth, Jade, I really don't want to talk about the show. I'm kind of tired. I've got a big delivery run to do today after school and about a ton of homework I haven't done." He looked at her briefly, then glanced away.

Jade felt a flush creep over her face. She started to turn away, then looked back at him pleadingly.

But David had a stern, slightly reproachful look in his eyes—a look that told her he clearly wasn't ready to make up. There was nothing she could do but walk away.

"Jade?" Elizabeth said softly, sliding into the seat next to her. They were at rehearsal, watching the chorus line go through their routine for the third time in a row.

Jade sat up and quickly tried to compose herself. She was feeling so rotten—so completely upset about David, and so glum about doing the show without him—that she could barely hide it. "Hi, Liz," she said, forcing a smile.

. "David isn't around, is he?" Elizabeth said. "I tried to find him today to talk to him about coming back to the show, but I couldn't find him anywhere."

Jade nodded. "Yeah, I wanted to talk to him, too. But he's really mad at me. I don't think there's any way that he'll reconsider doing the show. Not as long as I'm part of it."

Elizabeth gave her a sympathetic look. "You really think so? That's too bad. We're going to have to replace the set—DeeDee's working on it now." She patted Jade on the arm. "This must be really hard for you. I mean, it's probably the last thing you need. Just when you and David were starting to get to be really good friends— and with the show coming up on Friday night and everything."

Jade's lower lip trembled. "I'm pretty upset about it. The worst thing is that I can't even get David to talk to me so I can apologize. I said some pretty stupid things to him that I'm really ashamed of. I just wish. . . ." She paused for a second. "Elizabeth, can I tell you about what happened? Maybe you could give me some advice."

"Sure," Elizabeth said gently. "If you want to tell me, I'd be happy to try to help."

Jade slumped even further down in her chair. "Well, I think David got a bad impression of me because I handled all this stuff about my grandparents . . . like, I don't know, I was really ashamed of them. And then I blamed him for something he didn't do. And now David's completely disappointed in me."

"Why were you ashamed of them?" Elizabeth asked.

Jade shook her head. "I don't know why. I guess ever since I can remember I've wanted to be like everybody else. Like you and Jessica," she said admiringly.

Elizabeth stared at her. "*Why?* I'd give anything to come from a fascinating background like yours, Jade."

"Yeah, well . . . I guess I never considered it fascinating. I felt strange anytime people asked me about it. You don't know what it's like," Jade added, "having people ask you about China all the time. As if I'm supposed to know just because my family's from there. It would be so nice just to blend in, to be like the rest of the kids at school."

"But, Jade, people only ask because they're interested—not because they want to single you out as weird or anything," Elizabeth pointed out. "They just want to know more about China, and they hope you'll be able to tell them."

Jade sighed. "I guess so. I never thought of it that way before, but I'm beginning to see—you know, that I've been too defensive. That there *are* things I could tell them about. I'm just afraid it's too late for David and me. I don't think he'll ever forgive me for acting they way I did. I accused him of telling people about my grandparents' laundry, when—as he kept saying—it just wasn't such a big deal. Not a big deal at all."

"Well," Elizabeth said thoughtfully, "David is going to have to do some forgiving, that's all. He likes you a lot, and I think he'll be able to understand that you made a mistake. After all, everybody makes mistakes. And part of getting to know and care for someone else means learning how to forgive them when they're not perfect."

Jade had to disagree. The whole situation seemed so hopeless. "I don't think David will ever forgive me. Liz, you should have seen the look at his face when he came charging into the auditorium and tore down that set. You know how proud he was of it, how hard he'd worked on it. And then to just tear it all to pieces . . ."

Elizabeth nodded. "I couldn't believe he'd done it, either. But give him a chance to cool down, Jade. You never know what will happen."

Jade didn't answer. She was thinking that it was pretty unlikely that David was going to forgive her. She had messed everything up, and all she could do now was go ahead and give a great performance in the show.

That is, if her father would even let her!

Elizabeth found David in the cafeteria on Tuesday. She had spent all morning deciding whether or not she should interfere, and she was finally convinced it was time to talk to him. "Hi, David. Look, can you have lunch with me today?" she asked in a no-nonsense voice. "I'd really like to talk to you about the show. What do you say?"

David started to shake his head, but Elizabeth was ready for him. "I'm serious, David. We need to talk." And before he could object any further, Elizabeth took his arm and steered him over to a table in the corner.

"Look," she said, fixing him with an intent gaze as they sat down. "I know why you quit the show. Jade talked to me about the whole thing. Before I say anything about her, I want you to know how much *all* of us want you back. We miss you. More than that, we need you!"

"I don't want to talk about it," David protested.

"David," Elizabeth continued, "Jade's incredibly unhappy. She's been trying to find you since yesterday morning to apologize for what she said to you when you argued on Sunday. Why won't you give her a chance?"

"Listen, Liz," David said, looking solemn. "Ever since my dad moved out, I've been dealing with people being snobs about my mother's job. People making fun of me, people acting like we're not good enough for them because we don't have tons of money or status or something. And the only way I found to make my peace with it was to accept, once and for all, who I am, who my family is, and that what we *do* doesn't matter—it's who we are. And I realized more than anything else how much I love my mom and my whole family."

Elizabeth swallowed. "It must make it tough for you to sympathize with people like Jade, then," she said. "People who are still figuring stuff like that out, who don't have all the answers yet."

David looked at her uneasily. "You're making it sound like I haven't really given her a chance. That isn't fair. I really liked Jade a lot. I can't tell you how surprised I was by the way she was talking about her grandparents. It made me realize that she's completely different from the person I thought she was."

"Maybe you're jumping to conclusions the

same way Jade did," Elizabeth said gently. "Couldn't you try to help her? Couldn't you show her that she has a lot to be proud of in her family?"

David didn't answer right away. After a long silence he cleared his throat and said, "Elizabeth, Jade never gave me a chance. She wouldn't even go out on a date with me. Now that I've heard what her attitude toward her own grandparents is, I know why! She just doesn't want to be seen with me—she's ashamed of me, just like she's ashamed of them."

"David," Elizabeth said firmly, "Jade may be dealing with all kinds of pressures that you and I know nothing about. Her family is very conservative, very traditional. How do you know they even let her go out on dates?"

"I never thought of that," David admitted.

"All I'm saying is that you might be acting unfairly to Jade. Maybe you're assuming too much, being too hard on her," Elizabeth said. "She needs a friend right now, more than ever. Since you left the show she seems more and more tense. You're the one person she's been able to get close to."

David frowned. "I wish things were different, Liz. I really do. But after everything that happened last week, I'm not sure if Jade and I can still be friends."

* * *

123

Tuesday night Mrs. Wu slipped into her daughter's bedroom just before dinner. She told Jade that Dr. Wu had come home in a good mood and that she had asked him one last time about the show. He had said that he'd let Jade know at dinner.

Jade shrugged her shoulders. "Whatever he says is fine with me," she said listlessly. Actually, she almost hoped her father would forbid her to dance in public. Now that David had quit the show, she didn't really want to go ahead with it.

"Are you all right? Sweetheart, you seem upset." Mrs. Wu reached out to stroke her daughter's hair.

"I'm OK," Jade answered. "Let's go downstairs. Maybe there's something I can do to help with dinner."

When Dr. Wu sat down at the head of the table fifteen minutes later, he looked at Jade fondly.

"Jade, your mother tells me you really have your heart set on dancing in the show at school. Is that true?"

Jade nodded, keeping her eyes focused on her plate. *Not anymore*, she was thinking. But she could hardly say so to her father, after she had made such a big fuss.

"Well, I want you to know that I don't approve of it. On principle, I think dancing in

124

public is wrong. For anyone, and most of all for my own—my only—daughter. However . . . no man can stand up to pressure from two women. First your mother, then you, with your long looks. I don't think I can stand it anymore. So go ahead, Jade, and dance. But please forgive me if I don't come and watch. In my heart I still feel it's wrong, but I'm not going to hold you back. As your mother says, you're in America now, and I suppose I have to concede to some American values—although I can't personally embrace them."

Jade swallowed hard. She knew how much it had taken for her father to make such a big concession. And she knew she ought to be overjoyed.

But she couldn't feel that excited, no matter how hard she tried. It seemed like a hollow victory. Even thinking about the possibility of winning the dance internship in Los Angeles didn't make her feel better. David wouldn't be there to watch her dance, and neither would her father. So how could she possibly get excited about it?

Dr. Wu cleared his throat. "Eve, your dance teacher, called me today. She urged me to let you be in this show. She thinks you have real talent."

Jade tried to smile. She wanted him to know

how much she appreciated the effort he was making. "Father, I—" But her voice broke off. She couldn't possibly tell him what she was feeling.

So, she would be dancing on Friday night after all. But her heart wasn't in it anymore, and she couldn't imagine she would be anywhere near her best.

Eleven

Jade went through the rest of the week in a daze. She was experiencing so many conflicting emotions—first, relief that she'd be able to dance in the show, then sadness that David still hadn't forgiven her or made any attempts at reconciliation. And in addition to all this, for the first time in ages she felt close to her father. On Wednesday night he had actually asked about her rehearsal. And on Thursday he had asked a number of questions about the show: How long would Jade be dancing? How many people were expected to come? What would she be wearing?

The best thing was that she felt like her father wasn't trying to judge or condemn her with his questions. She felt that he really wanted to learn more about what she was doing.

"You know, Dad, you could come," she suggested on Thursday, the night of the dress rehearsal.

But Dr. Wu looked at her with a grave expression and shook his head. "No. It isn't right. But I want to know what it will be like."

Friday morning Jade woke up with butterflies in her stomach. The day of the show was finally here.

As she was getting dressed for school, she thought of the costume that she and Eve had chosen for that night, a rose-colored leotard, matching tights, and a filmy dance skirt—perfect for the flowing lines of the dance she and Eve had choreographed. Jade examined herself in the mirror. On the outside she looked the same: long, silky jet-black hair, almond-shaped dark eyes, and smooth skin. But on the inside she felt different. She felt—well, it was hard for her to explain it. But as she looked at herself she thought that she looked a lot like her mother and her grandmother. And for the first time in her life, she was glad.

Jade made a mental note to ask her grandmother the next time she saw her all about what it was like growing up in China as a little girl. Now that she had overcome her shame about her heritage, she was eager to learn as much as she could about her family's history.

When she came down for breakfast, she noticed that her father had lowered his newspaper and was regarding her. "Good luck tonight," he said gruffly. Then he gestured to something on the breakfast table. "That's for you."

Jade couldn't believe her eyes. A long-stemmed rose in a slender vase was sitting at her place. "Father . . ." she faltered.

But her father's expression warned her not to say any more.

All day long Jade thought about how nice it was of her father to have given her that rose. It made it easier to deal with the fact that she hadn't seen or talked to David since their fight.

At school the cast was incredibly excited, and the tension seemed to mount all day. Ms. Bellasario had decided that they would all meet for fruit and cheese before the show, to have a pep talk and generally calm everyone down before the big event. But Jade was too nervous to eat. Besides, she didn't like eating much before she danced.

"Remember I told you about that talent scout, Mr. Wicker? Well, he's here. And he'd like to

say hello to the dancers before the show starts,"
Ms. Bellasario said.

Jade felt butterflies again in her stomach. She would give anything for that internship. To dance with a real summer stock company—it sounded like a dream!

Mr. Wicker came backstage, where the dancers had assembled. He was a slender, well-groomed man in his early fifties. He was handsome enough, but he looked at all of them with an air that seemed condescending to Jade.

"Are these the dancers?" he boomed, rubbing his hands together and smiling at them. "I'm Mr. Wicker. And I'm going to be out in the audience tonight, watching you."

Amy Sutton batted her eyelashes as she introduced herself. "Mr. Wicker, my name is Amy. I've wanted to be a dancer forever and ever, I really have. I'm unbelievably dedicated."

Mr. Wicker beamed at her. "That's just the sort of thing I love to hear," he said. "Fine, fine. Well, I'll be right out in front tonight watching you all. I just wanted to come back here and wish you all luck. Break a leg!"

The minute he left, one of the sophomores in the chorus line turned to Jade and said, "He's going to be watching you especially, isn't he?"

Jade shivered with nervousness. She wanted to dance her best, but she didn't think she would be able to—not without David there.

In the dressing room Jade brushed her hair and clipped it back in the silver barrette Eve had given her as a good luck present. She had her costume on, and she knew she looked good. "I just have to relax," she told herself. Her palms felt sweaty, and her heart was beating fast. Taking a quick walk around backstage to calm down, Jade looked at the set DeeDee had made to replace David's—a board covered with different-colored flowers. It was pretty, but not nearly as special or dramatic as David's.

"What's wrong?" Elizabeth asked, walking up to Jade. "You look pale."

Jade swallowed hard. "Liz," she said in a low voice, "I don't know if I can go through with this."

Elizabeth patted her on the arm in support. "It's stage fright, that's all. You should see it out there! There's a huge audience, with lots of people you know. Everyone is really ready to have a wonderful time. I know you'll do fabulously, Jade."

Just then Cara Walker ducked backstage. "Guess what, you guys? David brought the set back. It's right there in the middle of the stage!"

Jade thought she must've heard wrong. David's set? Back? But she had seen him tear it down—in fact, tear it to pieces. How could it have gotten back? Unless . . .

Was that why DeeDee's set was still backstage? Could David have replaced hers with his own?

Holding her breath, Jade tiptoed into the wings and peeked out at the stage. There it was, as beautiful as before—the perfect stage set David had designed, a detail from the poster enlarged to display the beautiful form of a dancer in motion. But there was one difference. On the first backdrop Jade's face had been obscured. On this one she was smiling out at the audience, a serene, self-assured smile.

Jade felt her eyes fill with tears. She knew there was only one possible explanation: David had worked on the new set all week and brought it back tonight as a surprise, to let her know that he had forgiven her. Jade was suddenly overwhelmed by her feelings for him.

"Has anyone seen David?" she asked, turning back to the others in the cast. "I'd love to tell him how beautiful this is." Her voice trembled slightly.

"He must be out in the audience," Elizabeth said, patting Jade on the shoulder.

Jade could tell Elizabeth knew exactly how she felt. All the joy had suddenly come back into her life, and she knew she would be able to give her dancing her all.

The first part of the show went without a

hitch. The Droids played two songs, and were followed by a flute duet and a small jazz combo. Two seniors each sang solos. Then, after a short intermission, it was time for the serious dance part of the show. There would be routines, including the dance from *The Nutcracker*. Then Jade's solo, and finally the grand finale chorus line. At last it was Jade's turn to come out on stage.

Ms. Bellasario went out on stage to introduce her. "Ladies and gentlemen, tonight one of our sophomores, Jade Wu, will do the finale to our show. She'll be performing a dance that she choreographed herself, with the help of her dance teacher, Eve Miller."

Loud applause broke out, and Jade stepped out onto the stage. The lights dimmed briefly. It took her a moment to feel that she'd adjusted to them well enough to begin her routine.

Her eyes scanned the audience, quickly searching for David . . . and then, to her astonishment, her gaze landed on her mother. Clapping loudly, her face filled with pride, she was sitting right next to Jade's father, right there in the first row. And beside them were her grandparents and Eve, all of them watching her with joy in their eyes.

The minute she saw her father's face Jade knew she was going to dance like she had never danced before. She steadied herself, took a deep breath, and waited for the music to begin. And with the very first step she knew it was going to be the best performance she had ever given. She danced with a fluidity, a gracefulness that she had never attained before. She felt she was floating on top of the music—that she *was* the music. It was absolutely incredible, and she didn't ever want it to end.

When she finally sank down into a lovely bow, the entire auditorium went wild with applause. They were giving her a standing ovation!

Jade ran offstage and straight into Elizabeth's arms. "Go back out there," Elizabeth commanded. "They adored you! They're still clapping. Take another bow."

It turned out one more bow wasn't enough. Neither were two. Nothing stopped the applause— not until the whole cast came out to perform the grande finale chorus line. And even then the applause continued. When the performers took their bows, Ms. Bellasario came out and presented Jade with a dozen long-stemmed roses.

Jade felt as if her heart was going to burst. It had been the most perfect night of her whole life. And wherever she turned, she seemed to see David's stage set in front of her, the painted, graceful smile mirroring her own.

* * *

"Jade?" Dr. Wu walked backstage with a big smile on his face. "You were so wonderful." Jade's mother and grandparents were right behind him, and so was Eve.

Jade laughed with pleasure. "I thought you weren't going to come, Father. I was so happy when I saw you out there in the audience!"

"Well—" He looked around him with a smile. "I think I may have been somewhat harsh," he whispered to her. "Some of these people seem very nice. They clapped so hard when you danced, it made me think they weren't so bad after all." He put his arm around her. "I'm very proud of you, Jade."

Jade beamed at him. "Father, I'm so glad you came. And you too, Mother. And Eve, and Grandma and Grandpa. It made all the difference, knowing you were out there."

She heard the sound of a throat clearing behind her. When she turned around, she saw David, who looked almost as nervous as she had before the show.

"You were wonderful tonight," he said softly. "I just wanted to tell you how great I thought your dance was."

"Wasn't she great?" Dr. Wu smiled proudly, his arm still around Jade.

Jade stared from David to her parents and back again. "Uh . . . David, this is my father, Dr. Wu. And my mother." She hesitated, then said "Mother and Father this is David Prentiss. He designed that wonderful stage set you saw behind me when I danced."

"Oh!" Dr. Wu looked impressed. "You're a talented artist. I think the set is beautiful!"

"I had some help," David admitted. "From DeeDee Gordon." He took a deep breath. "But I'm glad you like it. I've wanted to be an artist for as long as I can remember. I guess for about as long as Jade has wanted to be a dancer."

"And are you musical, too?" Mrs. Wu asked politely.

"I appreciate dance. I like to watch ballet," David said shyly. Then he admitted to having a few part-time jobs that kept him too busy for other things, such as sports teams or music lessons.

Dr. Wu seemed very impressed. "That's a very unusual quality in someone your age. I like it when young people are responsible enough to take on jobs."

David smiled proudly. "I think it matters a lot, too," he said. There was silence for a minute, and David looked as if he were summoning up the courage to say something important. "I was wondering if I could ask you both"—he looked at Jade's parents as he paused—"if I could ask Jade out for dinner or a movie sometime. That is, if she wants to go with me."

"Good heavens. What a polite young man!" Dr. Wu exclaimed. He turned to Jade in astonishment. "I didn't know young men in this country ever bothered to talk to a girl's parents before asking her out on a date."

"Neither did I," Jade said, blushing. She was staring at David, her eyes moist. How had he guessed that this was exactly the right thing to do?

"If Jade would like to spend an evening with you," Dr. Wu began, "I certainly would have no objections. Would you?" He turned to Mrs. Wu, who shook her head and smiled. Then, after thanking Dr. and Mrs. Wu, David pulled Jade aside so he could talk to her privately.

Jade felt suddenly shy and tongue-tied, but David started talking. "You danced so beautifully tonight. I found myself thinking how much easier it is sometimes to express things without words. I thought your dance said so much about you. It showed so much grace, so much confidence about who you are and what you want." Jade's parents had moved away now, and David reached for Jade's hand. "I feel like I can only say half the things I want to say in my art. Don't try to tell me you're sorry, Jade. When I saw you dancing, that said it all."

Jade smiled gratefully at him. "Thank you for saying those things to my parents. You made everything a lot easier for me."

"So when do we finally get to go out? How about tomorrow night?" David asked, his fingers warm on hers.

"That sounds nice," Jade said softly. She felt as if a whole new world was opening up, and she barely knew what to think or do first.

Just then Mr. Wicker burst backstage, his eyes sparkling. "Where is Jade Wu? I need to see her right away!"

Everyone gathered around Jade, who was surprised to see Mr. Wicker. She had forgotten all about him in her excitement at seeing first her parents, then David in the audience.

But no one else had forgotten. An excited buzz broke out as everyone clustered around to hear what Mr. Wicker had to say.

"Rarely have I seen a girl of your age dance like that, and you obviously haven't even had rigorous formal training! Jade, you are a *very* talented young woman," Mr. Wicker said enthusiastically. "At first—I must admit it now—I didn't think I would be impressed. But the minute I saw you come out on stage, I knew you were exactly what we've been looking for."

Everyone gasped. Jade squeezed David's hand tightly.

"Jade," Mr. Wicker announced, his voice trembling a little with excitement. "I would like to nominate you for the Amelia Higginson Award for young talent and to ask you to dance as an intern with the L.A. Summer Stock Dance Company starting this June!''

An astonished hush fell over the entire cast and the friends and well-wishers who had gathered around. Jade had been selected for the coveted fellowship—it was really and truly hers alone!

Twelve

Mr. Wicker cleared his throat. "I hope you realize what a wonderful honor this internship is. Amelia Higginson is one of the most influential patrons of the arts in the entire community, if not all of Southern California," he said, pronouncing her name as if she were a celebrity. "You can imagine how many other girls would love to be in your position."

Dr. Wu came closer to Jade and put his arm around his daughter. "Can you tell us more about this internship?" he asked.

For just a moment Jade panicked. What if her father objected to the internship and refused to let her dance with the company? But as Mr.

Wicker explained what the internship entailed, Dr. Wu only looked prouder and prouder.

"And our Jade has won this prize?" he said.

Mr. Wicker nodded. "Of course, Miss Higginson herself gives the final verdict. But she always listens to what I say," he added hastily. "And I say your daughter has marvelous talent! She needs to be trained with the very best. It's time she got the attention she needs and deserves," he concluded.

Everyone clapped, and Jade closed her eyes for a brief second. "It seems too good to be true," she murmured. "I can hardly believe I'll be dancing with that company this summer—getting the chance to be in all those performances. . . ."

"There *is* just one thing," Mr. Wicker said, drawing the family aside so he could speak to them privately. "Amelia Higginson is from a terribly old, very established family. You know what I mean, don't you?"

Jade just looked at him blankly. "Not really."

"Well . . ." Mr. Wicker cleared his throat again, then looked around sheepishly. "I was just going to mention something about your name. You see, I think it would be better for all concerned if we presented your name to Miss Higginson as Jade . . . Warren, instead of Jade Wu." He coughed. "Much better anyway for the stage, for your future, don't you think? I'm sure you won't object to a tiny little thing like that."

Jade stared at him, her anger mounting. "Why wouldn't Miss Higginson like the name Wu?" she asked in a clear voice.

Mr. Wicker shifted his weight. "Now, let's not make a fuss," he said, lowering his voice. "You know how these eccentric old ladies can be. It's just a little quirk of hers, dear."

"But there must be a reason," Jade argued, looking straight at him. "Is it that she doesn't like names that sound ethnic?"

"Well . . . yes," Mr. Wicker said uncomfortably. "Of course, *I* don't feel that way. But we have to go along with the terms of the internship, and that's exactly what I think you should do. Just go along with it, for now. It's really nothing."

Jade was silent. She could see everyone in her family waiting for her reaction, along with Eve and David. Her parents were staring down at the floor, afraid to meet Jade's eyes.

And suddenly Jade realized that it *did* matter— a lot. If she were to go along with what Mr. Wicker said in front of all her friends and class-mates, what would they think? That she didn't have enough pride in her own heritage to insist on being called by her own name?

As the seconds ticked by, Mr. Wicker seemed more and more uncomfortable. "Please," he said.

"I need you to sign the acceptance form so I can take it to Miss Higginson." He looked directly at Jade. "This is a very important internship, dear. Your entire future could depend on it."

Jade stared at him. "Tell Miss Higginson," she said in a clear, firm voice, "that I accept prizes in my own name only. Jade Wu. Otherwise, I can't accept your prize, thank you very much."

Jade's words were greeted by a stunned silence.

"I hope you realize what a momentous decision this is," Mr. Wicker said coldly. "As I said, this internship could make your entire future. If you give it up—"

Jade stared at him, her head held high. "You haven't given me any choice," she said. "Everything I do, I do with my name. My family name. And that's all there is to it. I won't pretend to be something I'm not, Mr. Wicker. So I'm afraid I'm turning your internship down."

Mr. Wicker's face turned bright red. Then, exhaling a sigh of profound annoyance, he stomped out of the room.

Jade let go of David's hand and hugged both of her parents.

"That took a great deal of maturity, Jade. I can see how much that internship meant to you. I'm really proud of you," Dr. Wu said.

Jade didn't answer. Her eyes filled with tears.

That was one of the best things she had ever heard, her whole life long. Much better than any dance internship.

And now she knew she had done the right thing.

After the show Ms. Bellasario had arranged a cast party at Guido's, a favorite pizza parlor in town.

"Would you mind if I gave Jade a ride and brought her home?" David asked Dr. Wu.

Dr. Wu patted his daughter on the arm. "Jade has proven tonight that she's a young woman now, capable of making her own decisions. And I think she's shown very good judgment. You'll have to ask her what she thinks from now on."

David grinned. "OK, Jade. Will you let me give you a ride?"

Jade smiled back. "I'd like that," she said simply.

David and Jade had a wonderful time at Guido's. Jade—who hadn't eaten any dinner—discovered she was ravenous. She ate three huge slices of pizza and could have kept going! Now that she and David had relaxed and been honest with each other, it seemed that they could talk about everything. And everything made them laugh—especially Mr. Wicker. David did an imitation of him that caused Jade to burst out laughing. Then he started teasing her about how much pizza she had eaten.

"Quite an appetite for a girl your size," David joked.

"You try dancing like that," she scoffed, "and see how hungry *you* get!"

David put his hand over hers on the table. "Look, I don't want to get sappy or anything. I told you I'm not so great at words sometimes. But I want you to know, what you did backstage tonight—well, I was so proud of you! That took real courage."

Jade shook her head. "Look, there's no such thing as one internship making your career. If you're really and truly good, things will work out. I believe that. Now that the show is over, I'm going back to lessons with Eve every afternoon. Eve told me she knows some people in L.A. who run a dance company similar to Mr. Wicker's. And she might be able to get me an audition. So all's not lost."

"I'm sure it's not. Listen, after what I saw tonight—both onstage and backstage—I'm more convinced than ever that you've got what it takes to succeed."

Jade was quiet for a minute. "I'm sorry about what happened between us this week. It made me feel terrible. David, I really missed you."

145

His fingers tightened around hers. "It was my fault, too. It never occurred to me that you might have some reason for turning me down when I asked you out that had to do with you, and not with me. I was so sensitive about my own family problems that I never thought of yours. I hope you'll forgive me."

"Only on one condition," Jade said.

"What's that?"

"That you'll forgive me," Jade murmured.

David didn't answer her—at least not in words. Instead, he leaned over the table and kissed her. His lips were gentle and warm, and Jade felt her heartbeat quicken.

She knew he forgave her. More than that, that something very special was starting between them. Something brand-new, and very, very exciting.

"That," Mr. Wakefield said as he unlocked the back door, "was the best show I've seen. Everyone must have worked so hard!"

"It really was terrific," Mrs. Wakefield agreed, following him into the kitchen. "And thank heavens, Liz, now that it's over, you'll have a little bit of time for yourself again."

"And for Jeffrey!" Elizabeth grinned. "I think tonight was the first chance we got to be together in about two weeks."

Jessica was watching her father with great interest. "You know, Dad, I think you should think about taking dancing lessons. When I was watching Jade, I couldn't help thinking how great you'd look up on stage. Have you ever thought about modern dance?"

"Jess"—Mr. Wakefield groaned—"there's nothing modern about me. Haven't you discovered that yet? I'm just one hundred percent, good-old-fashioned father, through and through."

Mrs. Wakefield laughed. "Now, wait a minute. Does that mean you're through trying to feel young? No more exercise classes? No more flashy clothes?"

Jessica narrowed her eyes. "Yeah. Does that mean you're going to your reunion after all?"

Mr. Wakefield laughed. "Look, I may be old, but I'm not dumb. I'm not stupid enough to miss the point of your let's-make-Dad-miserable scheme. You spent the last two weeks trying to get me to realize that being young has its drawbacks—at least at my age."

Everyone laughed. "How'd you figure it out, Dad?" Elizabeth asked.

"I think somewhere between the Beach Disco and the exercise bike I got the idea." Mr. Wakefield shook his head. "Look, I know as much as the next guy that feeling young is all in the head. And I guess I learned a little bit of a lesson from Jade Wu tonight, too," he said, his voice becoming more serious.

"What lesson is that?" Elizabeth asked.

"Well, that sooner or later you have to make peace with who you are. Which means, for me, accepting the fact that it's been twenty-five years since I graduated from high school." Mr. Wakefield smiled. "And to tell the truth, being middle-aged isn't all that bad!"

Mrs. Wakefield put her arm around him. "I'm glad to hear it," she said. "I was afraid I was going to lose you there at the Beach Disco."

"Let's make some hot chocolate," Jessica cried. "I think we need to drink a toast to the new middle-aged Daddy!"

"Please," Mr. Wakefield said. "You don't need to rub it in. You never know when the urge to hear the Rats or whoever they were at the Beach Disco might come back."

"The Razors," Jessica said, frowning. "Not the Rats."

"Hot chocolate sounds delicious," Elizabeth said, getting the milk out of the refrigerator. "But I'd like to revise the toast. Not to middle-aged Daddy, but to parents who seem younger than anyone else's I know."

"Without losing their dignity, I hope," Mr. Wakefield amended.

The wink Mrs. Wakefield gave the twins made them both start laughing. "Dad," Jessica gasped in between giggles, "just promise us you'll burn that purple tie!"

"Well, I guess you'd have to call the show an unparalleled success," Cara remarked. A group of girls were sitting together at lunch, passing their slam books around and catching up on gossip now that the show was over. "We earned over six hundred dollars. Ms. Bellasario is thrilled!"

"Yeah," Amy said moodily, "but I can't believe Jade turned down that summer stock thing." Her eyes gleamed mischievously, as if she had a plan. "Maybe I should get in touch with that guy. If he's looking for someone with a traditional-sounding name, doesn't Sutton fit the bill?"

"I think Jade did the right thing. It took a lot of dignity," Cara said, ignoring Amy's idea.

Amy rolled her eyes. "If I hear one more word about that girl . . ." she threatened.

"I think we may have to put Jade and David down as Best-Looking New Couple," Lila chipped in, eager to make Amy even more irritated, as usual. "They haven't been separated once since the show ended!"

"Hey," Jessica said, her eyes focusing on someone across the lunchroom. "I've got a candidate for a new heading in my slam book—The Guy

Who Suddenly Has the Most Money, and Apparently From Out of Nowhere: Ronnie Edwards."

A silence followed Jessica's announcement. Ronnie Edwards certainly wasn't known for being well-off. His parents were divorced, and his father ran an all-night grocery store. Ronnie, who had curly red hair and brown eyes, was a member of Phi Epsilon, the fraternity at Sweet Valley High.

"I don't like Ronnie. I think he's a jerk," Cara said with uncharacteristic bluntness. "But you've got a good point, Jess. Since when does he have the money to come to school with all this fancy new stuff? Like that brand-new Walkman."

"And he's had new clothes on practically every day this week," Lila pointed out. "Not really *nice* new clothes, but they sure look more expensive than what he usually wears."

"Hmmm," Jessica said, her eyes narrowed in speculation. "Where do you suppose Ronnie's getting all this money?"

"Remember when Roger Barrett got adopted by the Patmans and turned into a millionaire overnight?" Cara asked.

Jessica shrugged. "Yeah, but no one's adopted Ronnie. He's the same old guy, just with a lot more money." Curious, but also suspicious, she watched Ronnie make his way around the lunchroom. "I don't know about you guys, but I intend to find out!"

150

Everyone at the table laughed. They knew that if Ronnie Edwards wasn't in trouble yet, he would be soon. There was nothing worse than having Jessica Wakefield decide she wanted to find out something! And from the look on her face, she obviously didn't intend to waste any time.

Coming soon: Sweet Valley High Super Thriller #3, **NO PLACE TO HIDE.** *When Nicholas Morrow falls in love with a beautiful girl named Barbara, he leads the Wakefield twins into their most dangerous mystery yet! Jessica and Elizabeth Wakefield are researching stories for the* **Sweet Valley News** *when they uncover some clues about Barbara's hidden past that seem to lead to a murder. Now,* **all** *of their lives are in jeopardy.*

How did Ronnie Edwards suddenly become so rich? Find out in Sweet Valley High #51, **AGAINST THE ODDS.**

☐ 26748	**NOWHERE TO RUN #25**	$2.75
☐ 27670	**HOSTAGE! #26**	$2.95
☐ 27885	**LOVESTRUCK #27**	$2.95
☐ 26825	**ALONE IN THE CROWD #28**	$2.75
☐ 25728	**BITTER RIVALS #29**	$2.50
☐ 25816	**JEALOUS LIES #30**	$2.50
☐ 27490	**TAKING SIDES #31**	$2.75
☐ 26113	**THE NEW JESSICA #32**	$2.75
☐ 27491	**STARTING OVER #33**	$2.75
☐ 27521	**FORBIDDEN LOVE #34**	$2.75
☐ 27666	**OUT OF CONTROL #35**	$2.95
☐ 26478	**LAST CHANCE #36**	$2.75
☐ 27884	**RUMORS #37**	$2.95
☐ 26568	**LEAVING HOME #38**	$2.75
☐ 26673	**SECRET ADMIRER #39**	$2.75
☐ 27692	**ON THE EDGE #40**	$2.95
☐ 27693	**OUTCAST #41**	$2.95
☐ 26951	**CAUGHT IN THE MIDDLE #42**	$2.95
☐ 27006	**HARD CHOICES #43**	$2.95
☐ 27064	**PRETENSES #44**	$2.95
☐ 27176	**FAMILY SECRETS #45**	$2.95
☐ 27278	**DECISIONS #46**	$2.95
☐ 27359	**TROUBLEMAKER #47**	$2.95

Prices and availability subject to change without notice.

Buy them at your local bookstore or use this page to order.

Bantam Books, Dept. SVH2, 414 East Golf Road, Des Plaines, IL 60016

Please send me the books I have checked above. I am enclosing $_____
(please add $2.00 to cover postage and handling). Send check or money order
—no cash or C.O.D.s please.

Mr/Ms _____

Address _____

City/State _____ Zip _____

SVH2—11/88

Please allow four to six weeks for delivery. This offer expires 5/89.

SUPER THRILLERS

YOUR OWN

Sweet Valley High

SLAM BOOK!

If you've read *Slambook Fever*, Sweet Valley High #48, you know that slam books are the rage at Sweet Valley High. Now *you* can have a slam book of your own! Make up your own categories, such as "Biggest Jock" or "Best Looking," and have your friends fill in the rest! There's a four-page calendar, horoscopes and questions most asked by Sweet Valley readers with answers from Elizabeth and Jessica

It's a must for SWEET VALLEY fans!

☐ 05496 FRANCINE PASCAL'S SWEET VALLEY HIGH
SLAM BOOK
Laurie Pascal Wenk $3.50

- -